VOICES
in the
DESERT

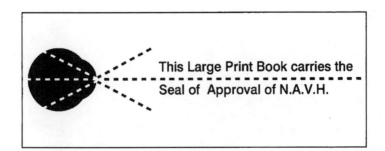

This Large Print Book carries the
Seal of Approval of N.A.V.H.

VOICES
in the
DESERT

Colleen L. Reece

Thorndike Press • Waterville, Maine

Published in 2006 by arrangement with Colleen L. Reece.

Thorndike Press® Large Print Christian Fiction.

The tree indicium is a trademark of Thorndike Press.

The text of this Large Print edition is unabridged.
Other aspects of the book may vary from the original edition.

Set in 16 pt. Plantin by Ramona Watson.

Printed in the United States on permanent paper.

Library of Congress Cataloging-in-Publication Data

Reece, Colleen L.
    Voices in the desert / by Colleen L. Reece. — Large print ed.
        p. cm. — (Proud heritage series ; 1) (Thorndike Press
    large print Christian fiction)
        ISBN 0-7862-8452-8 (lg. print : hc : alk. paper)
        1. Large type books. I. Title. II. Series.
    III. Thorndike Press large print Christian fiction series.
    PS3554.A4155V65 2006
    813'.54—dc22   2005036092

In memory of Alan,
who liked westerns

As the Founder/CEO of NAVH, the only national health agency solely devoted to those who, although not totally blind, have an eye disease which could lead to serious visual impairment, I am pleased to recognize Thorndike Press* as one of the leading publishers in the large print field.

Founded in 1954 in San Francisco to prepare large print textbooks for partially seeing children, NAVH became the pioneer and standard setting agency in the preparation of large type.

Today, those publishers who meet our standards carry the prestigious "Seal of Approval" indicating high quality large print. We are delighted that Thorndike Press is one of the publishers whose titles meet these standards. We are also pleased to recognize the significant contribution Thorndike Press is making in this important and growing field.

Lorraine H. Marchi, L.H.D.
Founder/CEO
NAVH

* Thorndike Press encompasses the following imprints: Thorndike, Wheeler, Walker and Large Print Press.

PART I
Jim

1

Jim Sutherland reined in his winded horse at the top of the rise and cursed him, ending with, "No-good crowbait. Should be left for the buzzards!"

Blackie snorted, breathing as heavily as the man he carried. It had been a long, hard climb up the overgrown trail. Both man and beast showed signs of strain.

Jim shivered and stared at the lopsided moon low in the sky. He grabbed his sides with his arms, as if to protect his body from the cold, spring night. Seven thousand feet. No wonder he panted.

"Fool!" he spat, knowing he lied to himself when he blamed the northern Arizona altitude for his weakness. Only too well did he recognize the signs that preceded the dreaded coughing spells he could not control. They started in the pit of his stomach, moved upwards, spread and spread until his body was wracked with pain. All the fighting in the world could not stop them.

It couldn't be far now. He had passed Daybreak hours ago. If he could hold on another hour he'd make the Triple S. He never should have chosen the shortcut. It looked as if it hadn't been used since he rode out five years before. Strange that Jon — he checked his thought as it started. The wracking cough threatened to defeat him just a few miles from the ranch.

"Not now!" His gasp was lost in tremors that shook his entire body and left him reeling in the saddle. He could taste the salty wetness of blood on his lips. His heart turned to ice. He could not stop now.

Blackie turned his head, peered at Jim, and took charge. So long as there was a trail ahead, even a dim trail, it was better to move than stand heaving while the man who had spurred him so cruelly on their long ride from Lee's Ferry shattered the peacefulness of the forest glade. Great white stars made ghostly shadows of frosty limbs and bushes. Blackie snorted again and headed down the trail. There must be something better ahead than this lonely trail and the cursing, coughing creature on his back.

Jim was dimly aware of when Blackie reached an open stretch and lengthened into a run. The coughing gradually sub-sided but with it went his remaining strength. He should pull Blackie in. He ineffectually yanked the reins but could not stop the now-terrified animal. Blackie swerved with the trail, rounded a bend, and rushed on. Jim saw the low-hanging branch too late, just as it neatly swept him out of the saddle and into a crumpled heap of agony. Was this the end? He tried to think. He'd come so far, couldn't he make it the rest of the way? Despair rode his shoulder as he tried to sit up and failed. He had to see Jon and Dad and Mother. He had to tell them . . . but he wasn't going to be able to let them know he'd been wrong. The oldest "Son of Thunder" was done for — and he wasn't even twenty-five years old.

Like cannon fire bursting around him, scenes Jim had forced himself to forget rushed over him, taking devilish advantage of his weakness. He could feel foam rising to his mouth and stuffed his kerchief over it. It was useless to struggle. He could not escape the past. He gave a mighty burst of effort, almost made it to a sitting position, then fell back on the needle-covered ground with an inarticulate cry. . . .

"We've got him!" Jim yelled exultantly. "Geronimo's trapped!"

"Just like a dozen times before," the soldier next to Jim sourly put in. "These Sierra Madres have more hiding places than a bee's got honeycomb."

"Not this time." Jim's sweat-streaked light-brown hair shone in the hot August sunlight, his brilliant-blue eyes lit with fanatic fire. "I tell you, he can't get away!" He gripped his rifle.

"That's enough of that!" The order crackled from their commanding officer. Unshaven, dirty, he reflected the state of his men after a long march. "We're to capture, not kill."

"Tell that to Geronimo," Jim muttered but the sharp ears of the C.O. heard him.

"You'll obey orders, Sutherland!" he snapped.

"Yes, sir." Jim Sutherland's lips curved in a snarl, but he turned away. In the months he'd been in the army he'd learned to curb his violent temper, at least in the presence of officers. The good old army way had to be observed at all costs.

Those costs had been great. Even now Jim's best friend Lester Thorne lay in a post hospital, dying from lung-shot. Jim shuddered. The lines of hatred deepened in his face. As far as he was concerned, dead Apaches were the only ones to be trusted. If he were in command he'd make short work of Geronimo and his followers. Their history of raiding settlers, escaping captivity, and raiding again was legend. Even after making a truce with General Crook this past March, Geronimo had escaped on the way to Fort Bowie, where he was being taken to prison.

Jim shook his head. The year 1886 would live forever in Arizona history as a bloody battlefield. How he hated Indians! He dropped against his pack and munched a piece of dried meat. Where had the hatred come from? Not from Dad. Matthew Sutherland always claimed Indians gave back just what they got. If you were square with them, you were treated the same. He'd proved it, too, back home. Jim shrugged. Navajos such as those in northern Arizona were a different story from Apaches. Kit Carson had rounded up most of the Navajos back in 1863, just after the Sutherlands came to Arizona. They'd been moved to Fort Sumner, in New Mexico. Four years later they were freed on condition they'd never fight again. They hadn't.

Their relatives the Apaches observed no such conditions. Tales of their burning and killing ran rampant. Sometimes Jim wondered — did they think scalping and raiding would keep out the hordes of settlers who were bound to come? Now that Utah was being populated, primarily by Mormons, other settlers would spill over into Arizona, the same way his parents had done years before. They had left the wagon train at Salt Lake City and headed south, never stopping until they reached the beautiful Kaibab Plateau, miles below the border. There they had literally carved their ranch out of the forest, using its trees and springs and grass for survival.

Jim bit into a hard biscuit — not much like those Mother made. A wave of homesickness left him angry. After five years, he should be able to forget that day he'd left home.

He couldn't. He could close his eyes and see Dad, forbidding and stern as he roared, "No son of mine is going to run off and fight Indians when the Triple S needs every hour of our lives! The Comstocks are lying ready to grab off our cattle in any way they can." His big fist shook the table. "And you," the accusing finger jabbed Jim in the chest, "you want to run off and join the army so you can fight Indians. There's going to be plenty of excitement right here, and you'll stay here, where you're needed!"

Jim's hair-trigger temper flared. "I'm

leaving — now. And I won't be back." He wheeled toward his twin brother Jon. "You understand, don't you? I want more than riding and hunting and herding cattle and being ordered what to do!"

The face so like his own shadowed. "You think you won't be under orders in the army?"

"At least I'll be my own man." All the love he felt for the twin who'd been part of him forever spilled into his voice. "Come with me, Jon. We'll show everyone. James and Jonathan Sutherland, 'Sons of Thunder,' like they called us when we were small."

"How dare you blaspheme in this house?" The Sutherland patriarch raised his shaggy gray head. His gray-steel eyes drilled through Jim. "You were named and nicknamed from the Holy Bible."

Jim's pleading eyes never left Jon's face. "Well?"

Regret darkened the matching blueness. "My place is here."

Aware of keen disappointment, Jim turned toward the door. "Good-bye, Mother, Dad." He hesitated but there was no word from his father, and his weeping mother was beyond speech. "Someday I'll be back." Five minutes later he pelted down the path leading to freedom as fast as his horse could run.

He had missed them more than he had thought possible. And Mescal — he could still see the skinny, pigtailed, openmouthed thirteen-year-old standing by the spring as he swept his sombrero in a low bow and called mockingly, "Grow up pretty, Mescal. I'll come back and marry you someday."

Her brown eyes had spit fire, and her black pigtails had bounced as she scooped up a large pine cone and hurled it with unerring aim. It glanced harmlessly off his arm, and he waved again before rounding the bend that hid her from sight. He and Jon had been six when Mrs. Ames stumbled to the Triple S from a nearby homestead. Her husband had been hurt while clearing land. By the time Matthew got there, he was dead.

The shock of it was too much for his frail wife, scarcely more than a girl. Just before sunset, she died, after giving birth to her not-yet-due baby girl. She smiled, whispered, "Mescal. After the blooming cactus," and closed her eyes, leaving the tiny baby to become daughter and sister to complete the Sutherland family.

"Move out!" The order jerked Jim back to the present, with a grin still on his face as he thought how Mescal had been well named. Frail as the mother had been, the

16

daughter thrived, until she was sturdy as the plant and sometimes as prickly when teased.

Jim clutched his rifle, scrambling to his feet. When the C.O. gave an order, it meant *now.*

"Look out!" The shouted warning came as Jim stretched cramped muscles — and too late. A rifle cracked, answered by a volley, and a "got him!" Jim was lifted from the saddle as if by a giant hand. At first there was no pain, just the sensation of having had his chest cave in. He glanced down. A neat hole in his shirt was rapidly reddening.

"Here!" The strong hands of the man next to him ripped open the shirt. Blood poured from the bullet hole.

"Did it go clear through?" Jim demanded.

"Yes." The soldier ran his hand under Jim's back, snatched the scarf from his throat and stuffed it over the wound, then did the same in front. "It's clean."

Jim coughed and tasted the sickish-sweet taste of blood. "Must have nicked the lung."

"Sure." The soldier's white face belied his hearty tone and the look in his face, and Jim closed his eyes against them, remembering Thorne, who'd been shot the same way. Somewhere there was more shooting, but he didn't care. He was so hot, and it was hard to breathe. When they came to put him in the hospital wagon, he fell mercifully unconscious.

He awoke in a cot next to Thorne.

"Hey, old man, glad you're awake."

Jim stared at his comrade's too-bright eyes, too-red cheeks. Was Thorne a living image of what he himself would become? He turned away, strangely apathetic. All he wanted to do was rest.

Time became meaningless, swimming by until Jim neither knew nor cared what day, week, or month it was. Even when word came in that Geronimo had surrendered in Skeleton Canyon and the war was over, Jim lay in a stupor. He and Thorne had been moved to Phoenix, where they were supposed to get better care. Yet when Jim tried to pin down overworked doctors, he was brusquely told, "Rest. It's all you can do." He alternated between despair and hope as his fever rose and fell. Sometimes he laughed bitterly. This was the freedom he'd craved? He was strong, muscular, trained for endurance since childhood and hardened by army life. Could one redskin bullet fell him? Impossible!

The following weeks brought little change. The fever came and went, the coughing spells continued, and he accepted the truth: He was going to die in this stinking hospital. The same way Thorne died the day before. They hadn't wanted him to know. The doctors mumbled something about moving him to another room for special care, but Jim knew better. During the long afternoon, Jim stared out the small window in his new room. There was a mescal plant outside. It accused him the way the child Mescal had done when Jim impatiently threw down his fishing pole because he wasn't catching anything.

"Quitter," she taunted. He'd stalked off, and Mescal had grabbed the pole, sitting hour after hour in one spot — and triumphantly bringing home a mess of mouth-watering speckled trout.

The suffering man groaned. Why should he feel her eyes staring from the past, haunting him with the assurance *she* wouldn't quit, no matter what the odds were against her? What choice did he have? He was going to die.

It burst in his brain the way he'd seen overheated cans burst over a campfire — nothing said he had to die here. He could go home, back to juniper and pine and sweet cedar, to welcome springs and rugged mountains and canyons filled with game.

His elation gave way to defeat. They would never let him go.

"So what?" he grimly demanded of the innocent mescal plant. "So I'm going, and no one's going to stop me. They won't drag a deserter back to die when he's practically dead anyway."

Twin spots of red crept into his cheeks, and his eyes glittered. He stifled a cough, plotting and conniving how he could get away. He must not waste strength arguing or getting permission. He would need every ounce of what little remaining grit he had to get to the home that had grown infinitely precious, now that he knew it might be lost to him forever.

All winter Jim lay in his bed when others were around and forced himself to get up and move until his coughing spells stopped him when alone. He stuffed down all the food they gave him. He closed his eyes a dozen times a day and conjured pictures of himself riding home. He feigned even more sullenness than he felt, and the hospital staff was glad enough to let him alone. His outer wounds had healed. Unless he overdid, they would stay healed. It was just that terrible sloughing away and harsh grip on his lungs that prevented him from springing from the bed and rushing off.

Spring came early. With it came cold knowledge — if he was to go, it must be now. He had fooled himself over the winter, fed by the hope of home. No longer. He was at his peak.

He left the next morning at 4:00 a.m., the hour when men's bodies are at their lowest ebb. He stole past sleeping men, hearing their snores and low groans, carrying boots in one hand, sombrero in the other. No uniform for him, to be discovered. Jim had seen them bring in a patient about his size days ago. When they had undressed him and hurried him off, Jim had silently slipped to the discarded clothing and hid it under his mattress. He had laughed when he heard them wondering where the dusty clothes had gone and finally decided someone had discarded them as worthless.

It felt good to be back in rough clothing instead of army issue. Jim felt his way, hoping no one would waken. The greatest danger was by the front door, where a dozing doctor sat. Jim crouched in a corner, then with an unaccustomed prayer that he would not cough, he crept forward

— one cautious step after another, the way he had crept past enemies so many times when he knew he was outnumbered and his only hope of safety was to escape undetected. Now that doctor was his enemy, to be outwitted by skill and stealth.

The doctor stirred.

Jim froze.

The next moment the doctor's tired head dropped back over his reports, and Jim was free to slip out the partially open door. He didn't dare breathe too freely for fear of the cough, but odors that had been dulled by hospital smells called him: a pungent bit of crushed sagebrush; the sharp tang of a hard-ridden horse; the coolness of a night wind, born in some faraway mountain, sweeping across the desert.

The clank of arms sent him hurrying behind a twisted tree. "Sir, a patient is missing." The doctor's low call turned the night unfriendly, and Jim shivered in the shadows. How could they have discovered him so soon?

"Which patient?" The speakers were so close Jim could see the tired lines on the doctor's face, the glint of metal on the officer's uniform. His heart pounded until it seemed incredible they didn't hear it.

"Sutherland."

The officer sighed, looked out across the desert, back to the doctor. "What chance has he?"

"None, sir."

"Poor devil. Don't bother reporting him."

"Sir?" The doctor echoed Jim's surprise.

"I've seen him look across the desert as if he heard voices. If he has to die, let it be where he chooses." He saluted smartly and walked away.

Jim smiled, but his eyes stung. He had just heard his death sentence spoken aloud for the first time and with no more feeling than someone passing the time of day. There were far greater things to consider than what he already knew. He had planned carefully. He would somehow get a little way out of town and hail the Prescott and Phoenix Stage. It took thirty hours to Prescott. From there he could get a ride with someone going north to Flagstaff, a mail or freight wagon, then another to Lee's Ferry. That would put him about seventy-odd miles from home. Could he ride that far?

He set his lips in a thin line. He had to. Lee's Ferry would be the only place he could borrow a horse. Those miles were going to be long. There were the Vermilion

Cliffs and House Rock Valley in between.

He started his long walk to where he planned to catch the stage. Time enough to worry later about the ride home.

Every jolt of the stagecoach ride was hell. Jim kept his eyes closed and concentrated to keep from groaning aloud in front of the other passengers. He staggered off at Prescott and barely managed to get to a hotel, where he holed up two days before going on.

The wagon ride on to Lee's Ferry was worse. But as his strength waned, his determination waxed. He borrowed the best of a bad lot of horses and started home, stopping only when he knew to go on would be to fall senseless. He pushed and strained, seated drunkenly at times, swaying at others, laughing foolishly when the fever came. Until the tree branch caught him. . . .

Jim opened his eyes. Blackie was nowhere in sight. The silly moon and oversize stars had been replaced by streaks of early dawn. He flexed his muscles, gingerly sat up, and felt the familiar tearing in his chest.

"To be so near and yet so far!" He coughed until he retched. Spent, trem-

24

bling, he fell back against the pine that had unseated him. He lay until his body stilled; then with superhuman strength, born of the iron will that had entered his very soul, he stood. His vision blurred from sheer weakness. Something moved, and he shut his eyes hard before reopening them and focusing on the clearing ahead.

A buckskin-clad Apache stood not fifty feet away.

Jim flung himself to the ground, clawing for the Colt revolver that had slipped from his holster when he writhed with coughing. His hands found it, cocked, aimed. The Apache was almost on him, coming at a dead run.

Jim pulled the trigger, but another seizure wracked him, and the bullet went wild. He was clutched by talon hands whose fingers bit into his shoulders. His Colt fell to the ground, and the Apache kicked it away.

"Jon!" The black eyes stared into his own and their expression slowly changed to something unreadable. "No. You are the other one." The Indian's gaze roved over Jim's sorry appearance. "The black horse is yours?"

"Who are you?" Jim tore free. "What are you doing here?"

25

Incredible scorn swept over the formerly impassive face. "I am Apache." He rose and towered over Jim.

Even through Jim's anger and pain he could not help noticing the perfect English and the statuesqueness of the bronzed man above him. Apache stood close to Jim's own six-foot height but was more muscular. Long black hair fell past his shoulders and was caught back with a band. His buckskins and knee-high moccasins fit as if molded to him.

"You called me Jon." Jim's brain whirled. Apache made no move to harm him. What was he doing this far north? He must know the Sutherlands — he had changed *Jon* to "the other one."

"Come." Apache reached down a strong hand.

Hating himself for accepting an Indian's help, but powerless to get up alone, Jim grudgingly stood to his feet and brushed the hand aside.

Apache gave him a contemptuous glance and ordered, "Wait here," before disappearing into the trees.

Jim slumped against the mighty pine's lightning-scarred trunk, glad of the rest. His struggle and exertion had just about finished him. His face contorted. A spurt of hatred brought his tired body erect. He would obey no Indian! He would get home on his own, if he had to crawl. It was too ironic to be dragged home half-dead by an Apache. He would tell them what another Apache had done to their son and watch their revulsion against this savage who gave orders like General Crook.

He took a single step forward and was stopped by the sound of hoofbeats. Apache crossed the clearing, with Blackie trotting behind him. The big Indian ignored Jim's curses and swept him into the saddle the way he would still a protesting child.

Jim was nearer fainting than he'd ever been in his life, but the ignominy of being dumped into the saddle gave him strength to blaze out, "I don't know who you are or what you're doing here, but you're still nothing but a stinking Apache, and I hate your guts!"

The Indian's control was superb. "The feeling is returned."

If the stagecoach and wagon rides had been hell, that last mile was damnation. It was all Jim could do to remain seated. His anger had taken a terrible toll on his fading stamina. Only pride kept him on the horse. He suffered tortures, although Apache carefully led Blackie at a walk. Jim would not sprawl at the feet of his arrogant captor. Neither would he cry out. The blood on his lips, when they rounded the last bend, was not from his lungs, but from biting his lips to hold back screams as knives tore through him, bringing anguish.

"Stop here," he commanded.

He was rewarded with an eagle-swift look from Apache and a curt order to Blackie. Jim made no attempt to explain. Yet he knew when he crossed the threshold of the log house fifty yards ahead, it would be for the last time. He would fall into a bed, die, and emerge in a pine box, to be buried somewhere on the Triple S. So when he stepped inside, he must carry a sharp enough memory of the home he had ridden away from so eagerly and had now sought to die in, to last the minutes and hours until it happened.

A great gasp of relief belched from his throat. Nothing had changed. The peeled logs were a little darker, and the trees and flowers were taller, but everything else was the same: Haunting Spring, which never went dry, was swollen now with its burden of melted snow-water; the dusty corral held a dozen horses; the barns; the rambling bunkhouse, where he'd played cards with the hands. A patina of early morning sunlight lay over it all, dappling through billowing white clouds that promised rain.

And the smell! Nothing on earth smelled like the resinous Ponderosa pines guarding the ranch like standing sentinels.

A curl of smoke lazily crawled from the rock chimney, and the smell of frying ham and wood smoke assailed Jim's nostrils, stinging his throat. What an utter fool he had been. Could any man ask for more than this? Yet he had chosen to go — now all that was left of him had come back, when it was too late.

A golden avalanche of frenzied barking shattered his bitter reflections. The collie raced around the corral and across the yard, straighter than a speeding, whining bullet on its path.

Jim's mind refused to accept what he saw. For a moment he was a boy again, beating Jon in races, but never their dog.

"Gold Dust?" Jim shouted incredulously.

The collie was closer now, leaping and bounding.

Jim tumbled from Blackie and met Gold Dust in a mighty embrace on the pine-needle ground, as they had done so many times before. Wounds, impending death, even the hated Apache above him were nothing to Jim Sutherland. His only reality was the ecstatic collie, the pet he had long thought dead.

2

"What's wrong with that animal?" The stentorian yell came from the open doorway.

Jim raised his head and gazed across the yard at his father, scarcely daring to look. Another wave of relief hit him. Dad had not changed. Tall, massive, he filled the wide door then stepped lightly off the board porch, piercing gray eyes and light step proclaiming him as the woodsman he was.

Before Apache could answer, a strong voice called, "Gold Dust hasn't acted that way since Jim left! You don't suppose...." A replica of what Jim had been before the last battle ran from the barn and outdistanced his father. Immediately behind him was a full-bosomed, black-haired young woman, lissome, but with the same brown eyes that had haunted Jim in his hospital room. Mescal!

But his attention strayed. A slender woman appeared in the doorway. "What is it, Matthew?"

Pain that had nothing to do with lung-shot flooded Jim as he crouched by his dog. The figure in the brown linsey-woolsey dress must be Mother, but how could it be? Mother's hair had been brown as fallen leaves after rain; this woman's was snow white. Yet as she came closer he saw the brilliant blue eyes her sons had inherited. It was she.

Jon reached the cringing, huddling figure, stricken with shame over what he had done to his mother, bitterly regretting the stubbornness that had prevented him from even writing. Gall and wormwood threatened to finish in Jim Sutherland what the bullet had started.

"It's —" Jon let out a whoop, reached for his twin, wild gladness in every line of his body. "Mother, Jim has come home!"

"Wait," Jim breathed, wanting them to warn Mother before she saw what a wreck he was. He desperately struggled to get up. He must be on his feet and meet her like a man.

It was too late.

"God in heaven, my son!"

Her white face matched her hair and gleamed in the sunlight as she ran to fall on her knees before her prodigal Son of Thunder. Joyous welcome turned to horror at sight of his hollow cheeks, bright eyes, and bloody shirt and kerchief. *"Jim!"* She seized his hands with a grip that would never again let him go. *"What have they done to you?"*

He buried his face in her calico-aproned lap as he had done so many times in the past when confessing a childish wrong and asking for forgiveness. Years fell away. He felt her hand move to his shock of roughened hair and remembered the gesture had always signified all was well.

He no longer had to pretend. Mortally wounded man dissolved into small boy as he clutched the wind-dried apron that carried the smell of comfort. He raised his head. A terrible cry of remorse tore from his innermost soul. "Mother — I've come home to die."

Silence pounded in Jim's ears. His body burned with shame like the Painted Desert in August. He could not lift his head to face Jon and his father after that cowardly cry. In all the battles he had never showed yellow. Now he curled into his misery, made worse by his own craven cry.

A contemptuous drawl cut the heavy air. "So you're still a quitter."

"Mescal!" Matthew Sutherland's roar as he whipped toward the sneering girl

brought Jim to his senses. He threw back his head. Hatred shot from his eyes. *"What did you say?"*

Her lips curled. She opened her mouth.

"Be silent, girl," Dad thundered, raising one mighty arm.

"Dad, no!" Jon sprang forward. "You'd not strike Mescal!"

Jim fought the red haze filming his murderous eyes. "Let her speak," he panted. Heart raw from his own cowardice, he felt even his lips turn white beneath her steady gaze. "If she knew the hell I went through even to get home, she wouldn't stand there like that." Memory of his agony roughened his voice.

"So it wasn't easy." Mescal didn't give an inch. "You made it, didn't you? Now are you going to lie there and die or get up and fight like a man? God help your regiment if you were no braver then than now."

Dad struggled for words that wouldn't come, but Mescal stepped closer. Jim could see tiny golden flecks in the depths of her challenging eyes.

"When you rode off, you told me to grow up pretty, and someday you'd come back and marry me." She swept him a slow glance, from worn, dusty boots to tossed brown hair. "You cut a mighty fine figure for a bridegroom, don't you?" Every deadly word struck like a bullet. In a pool of disbelief, she turned on her heel and ran into the woods.

"Don't pay her any attention." Jon's hoarse voice ended the ugly scene and he helped Jim stand. "She didn't mean it."

"She meant every word." Jim leaned on his twin, sweat standing on his forehead in great drops. He glared at the path Mescal had taken, then at the silent, watching Apache. The spleen he hadn't been able to muster to blast Mescal erupted. "You agree with her, don't you?" Foam coated his lips. "You think she's right about me."

A sardonic smile flickered across the set face. "I am only an Apache. What right have I to think or feel?" The swaying aspens parted, and Apache disappeared between them.

"Why is he here?" Jim ranted. "I come home shot to pieces by Apaches and find one in my front yard!"

"He's our friend." Jon picked up his brother and headed for the log house, ignoring Jim's protests. Jim was vaguely aware of being laid on a cool bed, stripped, and bathed. He turned away from the broth Mother brought, but gulped the icy water he'd dreamed of in the five years of desert and mountain fighting, too tired to care for any of them, even Apache.

He never knew how long his semi-conscious state lasted. At times he was red-hot, hearing shouts of Indians on the war-path. That was followed by trembling, cold shudders that even woolen blankets couldn't stop. Once he knew it was all over. Then a girl's voice rang in his ears, "Quitter . . . , quitter . . . , quitter." He gave a great heave of his body, and the murky depths drowning him receded.

One day he opened his eyes, too listless to move. The log walls of his old room smiled with sunlight from the open window.

"Decided to wake up, old man?" Jim saw in Jon's clear eyes the strain of what had passed. "Don't talk. Rest."

Jim's lips twisted. That's what the army doctors had told him. He stretched, aware of his terrible weakness. "How long?"

"Three weeks." Jon's blinding-white smile lit his whole face. He turned to the open doorway. "Mescal, bring broth."

"Don't let her in here." Jim shrank from his tormentor's presence. He might as well have saved his breath. Mescal seated herself in a chair hewn from a great tree and forced him to take the broth. He could see a faintly scornful twist to her drooping lips and faint blue shadows under her eyes. Aloof, silent, she slipped from the room as quietly as she had come.

"She hasn't been in here, has she?"

Jon's answer was succinct and betraying. "Day and night."

"Why? To see me crawl again?"

"You didn't crawl. No more talk now." Jon pressed Jim back against the pillow and followed Mescal.

Well, at least he wasn't dead, even if he was dog tired. Maybe there'd be a better time before it got him. He hoped so. He'd give anything just to go fishing once more. Jim sighed. That long trip home had taken a heavy toll. His thin hands plucked the patchwork quilt nervously, and when he heard Apache's low voice outside the window, his fingers curled into balls of hate.

One sunny morning Jon insisted on getting him into a chair. Panting with the unaccustomed exertion, Jim fell against the blanketed back. "What a miserable wretch I am!" He glanced through the open window and froze at sight of Apache. "Why's that snake hanging around?"

"Because of Mescal."

Jim's lips curled in disgust. "In love with her?"

The old fire Jim used to try to strike from gentler Jon blazed into a forest inferno. "Don't be a fool! Of course Apache isn't in love with her." The fire died to smouldering. "I'm the one who's in love with Mescal."

"You?" Jim felt jolted. "Since when?"

"Since always." Jon measured Jim with narrowed eyes that still held ignited sparks. "I used to think you'd be my competition."

"Not for that wildcat!"

"She isn't a wildcat all the time." Jon's eyes glowed like twin mountain lakes. "She's wild and sweet and true. Every animal on the place comes at her call. She's made pets of coons and crows and deer. She can't pass a wounded creature. That's how we got Apache."

Jim's breath quickened.

"Last fall Mescal visited in Daybreak." A shadow crossed Jon's usually sunny face, and his big hands lay curiously clenched. "She doesn't often get away from the ranch, but Alice Johnson asked Mescal in for a dance and over Sunday, and Dad finally said she could go. I was going to take her, but she laughed at the idea. Said she could take care of herself." Jon broke off with a rousing laugh that brought a smile to Jim's lips, in spite of himself.

"She can, too." Jon laughed again. "She can outride and outshoot Dad and me. In a contest between you, I'd be hard put to know where to lay my bet."

"That's pretty easy now," Jim threw in sourly.

"I mean when you get well."

Jim thrust back a pang at Jon's confidence. Even though he was undeniably better, he hadn't told his family of the continuing night sweats and spasms of coughing he muffled in his pillow. Good thing Jon was sleeping in the attic, instead of his own bed that stood across the room from Jim's as it had done for over twenty years.

"Go on." He couldn't keep the curtness back.

Jon's face shone with admiration. "Mescal left Daybreak early. She got halfway home and noticed a flock of circling buzzards off to her right. She's rescued fallen fawns many times, so she swung Shalimar toward the flock."

Jim could see her swinging off the main trail, as much a part of the big black as if she'd grown there.

"If she'd been another girl, she probably

would have run screaming from the spot. Apache had been dry-gulched and left to die."

Similar scenes rose in Jim's brain: blood-spattered golden leaves, isolated forest glades. Now he added a slender figure, bent over a fallen Apache.

"He'd been shot in the back five times. He'd lost so much blood he was nearly dead. Mescal didn't dare leave him and ride on home for us. Don't ask me how a slender girl like Mescal got Apache on Shalimar. I asked her once, and her face gleamed. 'I had no choice. I did what I had to do.' Anyway, she got him here. We took care of him and learned his story. He's only half Apache. His father was a white settler who fell in love with an Indian girl and actually married her."

"So that's why he speaks good English."

Jon nodded. "His real name's Charlie Campbell, but he won't use it. He says the whites have treated him even worse than the Apaches, who despise him for his mixed blood. He saw his mother killed in a surprise attack by the army. After Campbell deserted them, they were living in an Indian village." Jim's face darkened. "All the atrocities aren't on the Indians' side. Apache lay as if dead the whole time the

40

massacre went on. He's been roaming Arizona alone ever since."

Jim brushed the story aside impatiently. "So Mescal saved his life. That was months ago. What's he doing here now?"

"It's a good thing he was here, or you might not be."

Jim had the grace to look ashamed. "Yeah." He turned restlessly toward the window. Early spring had given way to warmer days, although nights were still cold. "Things look just the same, but they aren't. Here you are in love with Mescal. An Apache acts as if he owns the place. Mother's hair is white. Anything else I need to know? I'd just as soon not stumble on much more without some warning."

Jon rose to lounge in the doorway, straight and strong as Jim had once been. When he turned toward Jim, a softened, strange look mingled with the sunlight in which he stood. "When you get well, I'll be leaving the Triple S."

"I don't believe it!" Jim was aghast. "You've never wanted anything but the ranch! Why, after we were born, Dad changed the name from Circle S to Triple S to show the three of us were partners." His voice dropped. "After I left, I used to wonder if he'd change it to the Double S."

"He wouldn't and won't. Not even when I leave to become a minister."

Jim stared, then bent double, laughing until it made him cough. "You fooled me that time! For a second I thought you might be serious."

"I am." Jon's lips smiled, but his eyes remained grave.

"Never! We're the original Sons of Thunder, remember? James and Jon." Jim laughed again. "Although you never were the big noise I was."

"Not the original Sons of Thunder, just imitations. The original James and John were disciples — too." The last word was almost a whisper. Jon reached out a sturdy hand, pleading for understanding.

"But why?" Visions of tired, overworked, lonely men riding sagging horses as weary as themselves danced before Jim's eyes. "You'll give up all this you've worked for, to be a preacher? Why?"

"I've asked myself that a thousand times." Jon's brooding look witnessed how true it was. "Maybe it started in childhood, when Dad used to read to us." He picked up a worn Bible. "Remember Moses and Daniel and all those heroes? I always had to have a hero. The whole time we were growing up, you were my hero, leading while I followed, even though we were twins."

The controlled voice brought stinging hotness to Jim's eyelids. He had never known Jon idolized him.

"Then you were gone." Endless sadness filled Jon's voice, giving a hint as to how much he had missed his twin. "I had to find another hero. I did — in here. Someone to look up to and follow."

"Someone to replace me." Jealousy crept into Jim. "If you had to have another hero, why'd you pick someone out of the Bible? Why not Dad? Who is it? Peter? I remember him, always losing his temper."

"No, Jim. I picked Christ."

"Impossible!" Jim fixed a stony stare on Jon. "Jesus? That sissy who didn't have the guts to fight back when they killed him? You have to be loco."

"He was no sissy. Those hills in his country were no easier to climb than some around here." Jon's penetrating gaze never shifted. "What's the greatest thing you could do for me?"

"Why," caught off guard, Jim hesitated, blue eyes darkening to twilight purple. "Save your life, I guess."

"Suppose saving my life meant taking my place and dying yourself, so I could go on living?"

Jim squirmed. "Not many men would do that."

"One did." Jon laid the Bible back on the table.

"So now you think the only way to pay your debt is to be a preacher!" Jim's sense of loss harshened his accusation. A chasm deeper than the Grand Canyon of the Colorado had opened between them.

"There are many ways to pay a debt. Apache's way is to be here when Mescal needs him."

Jim's lightning-swift response was enough to change the subject. "Why should Mescal need a stinking half-breed? She's got you and Dad and —" his face went gray. He had almost added "and me."

"We can't be with her every minute."

"I would hope not. Much of her company would send a man screaming into the desert." Jim's curiosity mounted. "Why does someone who can ride and shoot the way you say she can need a bodyguard?"

"Do you remember Radford Comstock?"

Liquid fire ran through Jim's veins. "I'm not likely to forget that slick rustler and his thieving family."

"He's sworn to have Mescal. Been crazy over her since she turned fifteen. She hates him like poison. At the dance in Daybreak she cut him dead and, when he made a dirty remark, slapped his face so hard it sounded like a pistol shot."

"Good for her!" Blood sang in Jim's ears, despite his dislike for Mescal as she had been since he came back.

"Gossip has it Comstock's laid bets he'll have her if he has to drag her off behind a rope, the way he would any wild thing."

Contempt flared. "What have you done about it? Why haven't you and Dad ridden over and wiped out the whole bunch of them?"

"Dad doesn't know, and I hope he never finds out. That's just what the Comstocks are waiting for. If we ride over shooting, it will give them an excuse to pick us off — and you know what would happen to Mescal."

"Why doesn't the Daybreak marshal step in?"

Jon's eyes turned to molten metal. "He isn't likely to do that when his name's Radford Comstock and he's been put in office by his swarm of relatives."

"So that's how it is." Jim's mouth curved in a slow, unpleasant smile. "Maybe having Apache around isn't so bad after all, with Dad not knowing and you wanting to be a minister. Apache might just come in handy."

"Especially when it was the Comstocks who shot him, even though he could never prove it." Jon sighed. "I won't be going away until things settle down." Longing crept into his face.

"If it means that much to you, guess I'll have to put off dying for a while." Jim was rewarded by a smile like sunlight through fog. "What's Mescal think of becoming a preacher's wife?"

"I haven't told her how I feel." Jon confessed with a grin.

"Why?" Jim could feel the muscles of his neck cord. "Think she's too good for you?"

"No. I believe down past all the prickles she may love you, Jim." At Jim's speechless look, Jon added, "I think she took what you said five years ago a lot more seriously than you meant it."

"Now you're the fool," Jim snorted.

"Any other girl in your life? Besides Alice Johnson when you both were kids?"

Jim was tired of the conversation. "I've had a lot of time to think about girls where I've been, now haven't I?"

Jim's message seemed to get through. Jon stretched. "I've got work to do. Now that you're getting better, Dad's on me about letting things slack." He strode to the door again and hesitated. "Jim, if ever you and Mescal care for each other, don't let me stand in your way." His spurs clinked as he finished and was gone.

"Mescal!" Jim spat in disgust. Yet an hour later, when he saw her cross the yard, he measured her with new eyes — not as the childhood companion or the haughty stranger who flayed him with her tongue, but simply as a girl-turning-woman.

Sunlight caressed her curly dark hair and stained her smooth skin as she knelt to tussle Gold Dust. Her rounded body without an ounce of fat was in perfect, symmetrical proportion to her straight shoulders. The prickly attitude she maintained around Jim was strangely missing. In its place was the joy of youth and living that had characterized her since babyhood.

Her naturally red lips parted in a perfect smile. Even from that distance Jim caught the low gurgle of laughter in her slim, tanned throat as Gold Dust capered. Streaks of red colored her cheeks, and her pinned-up hair fell wildly about her like a black, cascading waterfall.

Jim caught his breath, and his sluggish blood stirred. She was beautiful. No wonder Jon loved her and Radford Comstock vowed to have her! Vaguely remembered feelings crept through him — feelings like those that died years before when Alice Johnson snootily turned him down for another escort. They struggled to be reborn, the way he watched butterflies kicking free.

On impulse Jim leaned through the open window. "Good morning, Mescal."

Her gaiety died. The flush of fun receded, along with her careless abandon in playing with Gold Dust. In vain the collie leaped and pawed and barked. Mescal straightened her simple cotton dress; the disdainful look Jim had learned to associate with her settled like a mask. "Good morning." She turned to smile at Apache, who had noiselessly stepped from the aspens.

Jim ground his teeth, unreasoning gall rising at the Indian whose presence he had barely begun to tolerate. Mescal must have said something to Apache, for he glanced at the window and Jim. For the first time a faint semblance of what might be called a smile touched his impassive face.

"By all that's holy, he'll pay for that!" Jim hissed through set teeth. "So will she."

All the long afternoon he sat in the chair by the window, seething with resentment at the girl who had once been like a sister, but who chose to befriend an Apache rather than be civil to her own kind. The longer he simmered, the more corroding became his hatred of Apache. By night he was trembling — and it ended in spasms of coughing worse than anything he'd had since his first week at home. This time there was no muffling it in a pillow. The fear in his parents' eyes was as real as the paroxysms that shook him. When they ended, most of his hard-won strength had been wrested from him, taking with it even the undying hope Jon had steadfastly clung to and cherished.

3

Why had he ever come home? Regret mingled with shame as Jim subsided from the coughing spell into familiar blackness. He had laid his plans well and carried them out, selfishly crawling home to die. Why hadn't he thought of what it would do to his family, having to watch his useless struggles? Mother, Dad, Jon, Mescal — her scornful face floated above him. She'd probably be glad enough to rid herself of his presence, since she thought he was a coward. Little snatches of memory: Mescal with Gold Dust; Mescal whispering with Apache; Mescal watching him with golden-flecked, contemptuous eyes — all combined in a whirl of frustrating helplessness shot through with pain.

Once he opened his eyes. Jon knelt by his bed. Jim struggled against the lump in his throat and weakly held out a wasted hand. It was instantly grasped by a hard, callused hand, and through the dimness of the turned-down-lamp lit room, Jon whispered, "Hold on, old man." The next time

Jim surfaced from the drowning pool of misery, Jon was gone. The room was still. He must have quieted down — even the lamp was out. Jon never would have left him unless he thought Jim had dropped into natural sleep.

Something slid in the shadows, and Jim's illness gave way to caution. It couldn't be Jon. He never moved furtively, as the indiscernible shadow did.

"Who's there?" Jim forced himself to a half-sitting position and strained his eyes.

There was no reply, just a curious movement that made Jim's blood ice and his skin crawl.

"I said, who's there?" But his demand dwindled to a whisper. Something about that black shadow was terrifying. Fear such as he'd never known before clutched Jim's throat. Was it death lurking in that corner, waiting, just waiting?

How ironic! Moments ago he'd been wishing he hadn't come home. Now he wished the entire family was with him. He sank back on his pillow in exhaustion, biting his lip until it bled. He would not show craven again. His fingers picked at the quilt. If death wanted him, let it step forward boldly.

"Come on, you —" He couldn't get the curse out.

This time there was an answer — no more than a current of air as a tall figure loomed over him. For a moment Jim braced himself, then automatically opened his mouth in a last cry for mercy. He was rewarded with a cloth roughly stuffed in his mouth.

Death wouldn't gag a man, would it? Jim fought strong arms lifting him from the bed and the cough that could go nowhere tearing inside him. His wildly flailing hands were stilled, but not before they contacted buckskin.

Apache!

But what was he doing — and why?

Jim struggled silently, furiously. He was overpowered as easily as Mescal might overpower an outraged kitten. The muscled arms lifted him, and Jim felt himself being carried. Red-hot anger burned inside, and again he fought, tearing out and striking blindly. Once he heard an involuntary grunt, quickly smothered.

Then they were outside.

It was starlight, and Jim's suspicions were confirmed. Apache carelessly tossed him into the saddle of a waiting, saddled and bridled horse. Shalimar! Jim heard the big black snort as ruthless hands tied him securely in the saddle.

If only he could get his hands free, get the gag from his mouth. Blue murder shot from his heart. Just one chance to sink his fingers into the treacherous throat of the Indian snake his family had saved, and he would die happy.

There was no chance. Apache crammed a sombrero on Jim's head, silently mounted King, Jim's gray stallion raised from a colt, and goaded him into a slow walk. Jim saw the long lead line between the two horses, noting how heavily packed King was.

What kind of evil scheme did Apache have in his half-white brain? Was he to carry Jim off somewhere and torture him even more than what Jim had already endured? What might happen while he remained in Apache's power? The thought brought great drops of sweat to the suffering man's forehead, despite the coldness of the night, and he strained against his bonds. He only succeeded in wearing himself into semiconsciousness. He slumped over, held in the saddle by ropes rather than will.

In the jumbled nightmare that followed their entrance into the aspen grove near Haunting Spring, voices screamed in Jim's ears. They must be part of what couldn't really be happening, he knew. Apache wouldn't dare creep in and abduct him! Once he thought he heard Mescal's voice in a low undertone. It was enough to rouse him from his stupor. Only the rustling of aspen leaves greening and whispering filled the air.

It was his last lucid thought. A heavy fog fell over him like a scratchy army blanket, and he knew no more.

Hours or days or centuries later, Jim opened his eyes. He lay on a carpet of pine needles, saddle propped behind him for a pillow. He could smell some strange, resinous odor that filled his nostrils with repugnance.

"Drink." The voice of his hated enemy mingled with the unwelcome smell, and Jim turned his head to see Apache bending over him with a battered cup.

With every ounce of strength he could muster, Jim struck out at his captor's hand. His puny blow didn't even spill the contents of the cup. It did bring a blaze to the usually imperturbable eyes. Apache deliberately knelt against Jim, pressing the defending arm into the ground. He tipped Jim's head back and lifted the cup to his lips. Jim obstinately closed his mouth.

Apache's hard lips curled, and he immediately pinched Jim's nostrils together tight.

Gasping for air, Jim opened his mouth, was met by a deluge of bitter herbs, and automatically swallowed again and again, until the cup was empty and Jim choking from the acrid, unpleasant taste.

"You see," Apache told him, "There is no use fighting. You will do what I say."

"I'll see you in hell first!" Jim panted, hands clutching the ground in an effort to keep from screaming.

"Probably. Just remember —" He paused as if to allow the significance to sink in. "Wherever I am, you'll be with me."

Jim spat at Apache's moccasins. The next instant his left cheek glowed from the hard slap Apache administered much as he would cuff a dog.

"You rotten, filthy Indian!" Jim tried to spring to his feet but only succeeded in starting another coughing spell in his rage. When it dwindled, he glared at Apache through red-rimmed, tear-streaked eyes. "Hit a dying man!" He couldn't spill out his venom.

"I do what is necessary." The bronzed face didn't move a muscle, and he sounded almost bored.

Hatred a thousand times greater than anything he'd ever felt exploded in Jim. "I'll kill you for that someday."

Apache sneered, his face turning cruel. "If you live long enough, which I doubt." For a single moment his eyes bored into Jim with a fanatic light. The sunlit glade darkened, although the sun still bravely pierced through the trees. "James Sutherland, the mighty, crawling on his belly, making threats! Don't you know you are yellow clear through?"

His accusation was like pouring vinegar on an open wound, irritating the already-guilty feeling Jim carried over his cowardice. He opened his mouth to scorch the devil before him but never got the chance. Apache seized him by the front of his coat and half dragged him to Shalimar. "You'll do what you're told and like it, *white man!*"

It was futile to protest, better to save what energy he had. Deep inside Jim, determination was born. He would watch and wait, and if the God Jon was planning to follow let him live long enough, Apache would have an unguarded second, and Jim would strike. He would think no more of killing the man retying him into the saddle than crushing a snake beneath his boot heel. Strength that had faded in spite of love for family was born anew by sheer hatred. There had to be a time. There would be. Jim would stay alive until there was.

Evening shadows deepened as they began their trek.

"Aren't you going to gag me?" Jim taunted.

"Why bother?" Apache's raised brows gave him an even more evil look. "You can scream yourself hoarse, and no one will hear you."

For the first time, Jim looked at his surroundings. Nothing to distinguish them from any other part of the Kaibab Plateau, except the change in trees from pine to cedar.

"Where are you taking me?"

This time a definite smile lit up the cruel bronzed face. "You said it earlier. To hell."

Jim cursed and turned away from the obvious enjoyment on Apache's face. The scrape of whiskers against his coat as he hunched lower in the saddle prompted a final question. "How long have we been gone?"

"Three days. For reasons I'm sure even a white man can understand, we are traveling nights only — and only part of them. It isn't my plan to push you into dying — yet."

Even Jim's anger couldn't ignore the sinister way Apache had stressed the word *yet*. He closed his lips and concentrated on staying conscious. At times he clenched his fists and chewed his lip to keep from pleading for rest. He was spared the final ignominy. At the exact time Jim knew he could go no farther, even tied as he was, Apache called a halt. There were more bitter herbs to be forced down him. Jim would not submit, and each time the same struggle occurred.

"Seems like you'd be smart enough to learn to give in," Apache settled back after still another tussle. He eyed Jim. "The sooner you learn who's boss, the easier it will be."

"Never! I'd rather be dead than give in to you, Indian."

"That isn't an alternative just now. If I'd told you back at the Triple S you could even come this far, you'd have thought I was lying." Apache's inscrutable eyes pierced to the weakest chink in Jim's armor. "Remarkable what one can do when he has to."

"I'm only staying alive to get a chance at you." Jim couldn't keep it back; all the hatred and anger spilled out in a rush.

"That's as good a reason as any." Apache

wasn't even disturbed. He merely threw more brush on the tiny, controlled fire and stretched to his full, superb height.

Yet even hatred and anger couldn't keep up forever. Jim got to the point where he no longer knew or cared what day it was. They had left the plateau. Cool forests had been traded for red rock canyons. Northern travel took an eastern turn. Where in the world was Apache taking him? Never had he seen land so desolate. Arizona Territory couldn't hold such places, could it, except deep inside the bowels of the Grand Canyon of the Colorado? The day came when they no longer traveled by night. Jim had long since given up wondering why Jon hadn't followed. Even if he'd tracked them at first, now that they painstakingly traveled over sheer red rock, no tracks could be left. There wasn't a soft spot for miles.

One day Apache disappeared. By late afternoon Jim had to admit there were worse things than being captive. Apache had been careful to drive off Shalimar, and Jim had no strength to find him. He lay on a blanket beneath a shelving of red rock, looking across a sluggish stream toward red buttes and cliffs and crags hundreds of feet high. Apache hadn't lied. Hell itself couldn't be worse. There wasn't a blade of green grass in sight. The only sign of life was a group of small lizards sunning themselves on the rocks.

Was this Apache's revenge? To pack him up here and leave him to starve? What a diabolical plot! All the fiends of hell couldn't have planned it better.

Bitterness eroded Jim's insides, and as the second day passed, he grew feverish. The water in the canteen was low. He had no taste for food. Why eat and prolong the agony? If there was a God, let Him send death quickly.

Jim's prayer, if it could be called such, was interrupted by a soft footfall.

Was it gladness that he wasn't alone that brought the strange cry to Jim's throat? Apache stood before him.

"Did you miss me, white man?"

The gladness was short-lived. Jim forced himself to respond. "Were you gone?"

Dark eyes, keen as a hawk's, swept over him. Apache deliberately laid one hand over Jim's breast and pressed. Nausea threatened to overwhelm Jim.

"It's time to move on." Apache drove forward two pack burros, heavily laden with supplies, whistled, and Shalimar and King appeared. Jim's eyes widened. Evidently their strange journey wasn't over. He submitted to being tied in the saddle again, sagging against his pinnings for support.

Deeper and deeper they went. Once Jim shuddered, thinking even a well man could never ride back out without Apache's guidance. There would be no escape that way. Too many tortuous turns, and canyons crossed and recrossed. Part of the time they rode up stony ways. At other times they were in a stream or river. Hard as he tried, Jim could not place where they could be. It must be somewhere in Utah. He'd watched the North Star enough to know they had left Arizona days before. Travel was slow, exhausting, draining Jim of all he had except his hatred and relief over not being alone.

When he was ready to give up, Apache's taunts kept him going. When he knew he was dying, Apache's bitter herbs lessened his cough but did not cure it. His beard had grown until it bothered him. He was used to being clean shaven.

The night Jim knew was his last followed a bad spell. Red rocks ranging from scarlet to crimson, which looked like spilled blood, swam together, and Apache had to carry him from Shalimar to a small cave.

Jim finally asked, "Aren't you afraid of what Jon will do?"

For a tense moment Apache searched him, as if holding back a last, terrible blow.

"Well?" Froth rimmed Jim's lips, making his blue eyes terrible in his wasted face.

"He will do nothing."

"You mean because he's going to be a preacher and is supposed to love enemies and all that rot?" Jim's cracked lips opened wide in a hoarse laugh. "Don't count on that protecting you!"

"I'm not." Apache had never been more impassive. "He thinks you didn't want to have them see you die, so I took you away."

"What?" The word cracked like a rifle shot. What new torture was this? Jim stared at Apache, who never moved a muscle.

"You are slow of understanding, weak one. They know you are brave, all except Mescal," Apache's mouth twisted, and Jim wanted to slam his fist into its mocking curves. "Isn't it what they'd expect of their Son of Thunder?" He laughed aloud, a harsh, grating sound that echoed and re-echoed between the cliffs frowning down at them.

Jim snatched at his words like a starving man at a crust. "All except Mescal?" He glared at his tormentor, whose face was even redder than usual, as the sun reflected from a vermilion cliff.

For the second time, Apache hesitated. Then he softly said, "Who do you think is behind all this?"

Incredulity, amazement, disbelief, and fear blended into a single word cry. "Mescal?"

Truth that could not be denied etched itself on the watching face. "Yes. Do you think I would choose to spend my time with you in this place?" His casually waved hand indicated the gloomy canyon walls and lack of life. "Mescal saved my life. I am repaying her."

"I don't believe you."

"Don't you, white man?" In one bound Apache was on his feet. "Then believe this. I do not lie. She planned it all. She begged me to take you away so they wouldn't have to see you die." Other words seemed to tremble on his carved lips, but they did not spill over. "Even I, Apache, would hardly have dared steal Shalimar and King, the choicest horses on the Triple S."

The blow left Jim reeling. "But why?"

"Who am I to know the secrets of white women's brains?" Apache shrugged and busied himself with making a fire. "Perhaps she knew it was too hard for your family. Perhaps she was tired of caring for you. Or perhaps she felt out here you would die like a man, not a sniveling coward."

"So you will bury me and carry word back," Jim jeered. "All about how Jim Sutherland gave up and died. Well, you —" He cursed softly and horribly. "It's not going to happen. Do you hear me? I'll lick you and this cursed place and this sickness. I'll go back and tell them you turned traitor, tortured me, and that I finally killed you in self-defense and buried you here!"

The sun had dropped behind the high cliff, and shadows covered the camp. From their depths came Apache's voice, "You have spoken. Now we will see if white man lies."

Spent by the revelation, brain revolving, Jim fell senseless to his blanket. It was the last clear thinking he did for a seemingly endless time period. He was vaguely conscious of being cared for, of food being given him, and at last, of being put back on Shalimar. During the ride, his mind cleared. Vegetation had begun to appear, growing out of the rock walls. He dimly noted the start of surprise Apache showed over something on the trail and forced heavy eyelids up long enough to note hoofprints. So they weren't the only ones left in this yawning, gaping, wounded world. It didn't seem to matter.

Since the last confrontation with Apache, Jim's hatred had been split. If Mescal could do this to him, what might she do to Jon? Even when the extreme coughing and demanding fever spells came, one thought burned and beat in his brain: He must save Jon. He must get well, tell Jon what Mescal was — and warn him about Apache.

After the telltale marks in the trail, Apache moved with caution. He drove them both until they were ready to drop. Even the hardy burros and horses showed fatigue. Only Apache himself gave no signs of weariness. If he ever slept, Jim didn't know when. Any time he awakened, the grim reminder of his captivity was there with watching eyes, like a vulture hovering over a dying animal.

The next day it suddenly ended. They rounded a bend and were confronted by the end of a box canyon. Narrowed to a few feet at one end, the only way out was the way they'd come in. In one of his conscious moments, Jim could laugh. "Not so smart after all, huh, redskin?"

Apache didn't slow his speed. He kept

riding along the crumbling ledge that narrowed, narrowed, until it disappeared into a gushing waterfall. Jim's jaw dropped as Apache rode directly *into the waterfall,* motioning Jim to follow. Not believing what he was doing, Jim let Shalimar pick his way after King and the burros. He blinked and tried to adjust his eyes from the glare of red canyons to the dim cave and passageway behind the still-rushing waterfall. His sluggish blood stirred. Step by step Shalimar found his way along the ledge above what seemed a large pool of water. Far ahead Jim saw a dim light that widened as they drew near. It must be the opening or entrance of the deep cave, hewn into the mountains of tortured rock.

At the opening he hesitated, unwilling to see what lay ahead. Perhaps this was just one more way Apache would make sure no one ever found his grave. The morbid thought brought a snarl to Jim's lips. He started to turn Shalimar and was stopped by an iron grip on the reins. Apache, on foot now, led the snorting black out the opening into the sunlight.

Jim could only stare.

Rimmed in by the bleeding rocks, as he mentally called them, lay a verdant fertile valley, perhaps a mile long and a little wider. A lazy stream wound its way through cottonwoods, showing the elevation was lower than where they'd been before. At the far end, King was already knee-deep in green grass, and the burros were standing, waiting to be unpacked so they could roll. Sage smell melted into pungency as Shalimar trod through it and wildflowers, after Apache.

"Welcome to paradise," Apache told him, inscrutable face turned toward the far side of the stream, where deer grazed unhurriedly.

"Where are we?" Jim demanded, turning a fierce glare on Apache. "One of us will be buried here. I hope you. It won't hurt for me to know now where you've brought me, will it?"

"Not at all." Apache was already engaged in throwing the packs from the burros. "We are in the Utah brakes and have followed the Paria River the last few miles. Before that it was Cottonwood Creek, which cuts the canyon through the Paria Plateau from northeast area of Kanab, in the Vermilion Cliffs. That's why some of the valley floor is two thousand feet below the rim." His strong hands stilled. "You are only the second person I know who has been here."

"And you were the first." Jim tore his

gaze free from the boxed-in valley surrounded by violent red cliffs. "Were you here before? You must have been, to find it!"

"No. My grandfather told about it. He learned of the hidden canyon and waterfall and valley from his father."

"You mean you brought me through all that twisting, turning trail without knowing where we were going?" Jim shook his fist at Apache.

"I knew."

His calmness enraged Jim. "You — you —" Words wouldn't come.

"Save your strength. You're going to need it for what we must do now."

"What do you mean by that?" Jim managed to slide from Shalimar, after Apache untied him. Menace hung in the peaceful valley where no fear should have been. Even the deer raised their heads, as if uncertain, then bounded a few feet away and resumed grazing.

Apache's closed face showed no emotion. He drew a razor-sharp knife from his belt and laid it on the ground. "I am going to open your wounds."

Thunderstruck, Jim couldn't move, but seconds later he threw himself to the ground and clawed for the knife. "You aren't carving on me, you red devil!" His nerveless fingers closed on the hilt but loosened as Apache's bone-crushing grip caught his wrist.

"I will do what I have to do." The cliffs above were no more feelingless than Apache's face.

"And let me bleed to death?" Jim choked out.

A faint smile touched the other's features as if a shadow had crossed the sun. "What's the difference? Bleed to death or cough to death?" He sighed and explained the way he would explain to a small, naughty child. "The wounds are healed on the outside but not the inside. By opening them up and letting the air in, they may heal inside. Of course, they may not. Either way, you don't have much to lose."

"You are not cutting me." Jim forced himself to stare directly into his Nemesis' face. "I won't give you the satisfaction of working me over and making me suffer more, then sitting there taunting me while I die."

Ice crystals tinkling against a window were no colder than Apache's words. They fell like heavy rocks into Jim's fear. "I thought by now you knew who was master. I was wrong."

Jim flinched in spite of himself. Raw reality faced him. He forced himself to keep his gaze steady, even when Apache drew back his mighty fist. He would not beg.

He felt a battering ram hit his jaw.

Then all went black.

4

Once, in childhood, Jim had heard someone speak of the seven devils. Now he knew it had been wrong. Those seven devils were multiplied into seventy thousand, all with the gloating face of Apache. They carried spears of glowing, red-hot, searing pain and thrust them into his body, leaving him writhing. Yet beaten into his brain was the cry, "No mercy. I will not cry for mercy." It shut his parched lips and sent blood into his throat, as he bit his cheeks to keep from screaming.

The sought-for periods of blessed unconsciousness in the abyss of darkness grew less. He was vaguely aware of the bitter herb drink forced into him and soft pads of wool pressed against the wounds Apache refused to let heal. During the day, unless they bled, Apache left them uncovered to the fresh air. Jim slept on a tarpaulin, face to the sky, his only covering against early summer storms the frail canvas Apache drew over his face when it rained.

By the time Jim could sit up without

knives tearing at his chest, weeks had been consumed. "What date is it?" he croaked against his will.

"Sometime in July."

Jim closed his eyes and slid back to the ground. He found it impossible to believe, but after a few days of watching the sun's path and noting how early its streams sought him out, he had to accept that Apache had spoken the truth.

He gritted his teeth. Apache! The cursed machine who never made a mistake. Not once had Apache slipped enough to leave a gun where Jim could seize it. If he had — Jim smiled grimly. Would he shoot Apache or himself? The morbidness of the question bored into him.

Apache broke his thought by stepping nearer. He had discarded his shirt and wore only buckskin breeches and moccasins. Sweat glistened on the copper skin, and a film of moisture obscured his set face. For the first time Jim saw telltale signs of the long vigil and its toll on his guard.

"Tomorrow you walk, white man."

Jim didn't answer. Caught up in his discovery, he paid little heed. Let him think he'd won. It would throw him off his vigilance and give Jim the opportunity he'd prayed for. "Whatever you say." He caught the quickly hidden flash of surprise in Apache's face and turned away to hide his elation.

When Apache got Jim to his feet, it was like teaching a newborn colt to stand, then take a few unsteady steps. Great drops burst forth on Jim's forehead, and he would have collapsed if it had not been for the rocklike support of Apache.

Jim fell to his tarp and blankets, wondering if he'd ever get up from them again. The next day he walked farther. Within a week he had stumbled as far as the stream, noticing it was down since they arrived. It was hot, boiling, miserably hot, and every step was misery. Only Apache's goading, "Is the little boy tired?" gave enough impetus for Jim to crawl back to his nest. Disheveled, filled with anger, he held his tongue and inwardly gloated about how he would pay that sneering devil.

The day came when Jim walked the length of the valley. When he returned, he threw himself facedown into the shrinking stream, reveling in its coolness. The water laved his hot face and arms and whispered the message, "You're well."

Startled, Jim could not believe the truth of it. The next moment he leaped up, tore free his shirt, and gazed at the healed wounds. He had known for days he was better. Now it was time for the final test. He deliberately gulped in great breaths of air, waiting for the too-familiar rending that always preceded coughing spells.

It didn't come.

He gulped again.

Again.

Only the hot, sage-scented air moved in and out of his lungs.

"Apache!" he screamed, forgetting all else but his miraculous news. "I'm well!" He flung his arms wide, raced across the valley, shouting, leaping into the air, a madman running wild in his ecstasy.

Apache rose from the fire beneath two neatly spitted rabbits. A rare smile lit his face for a fleeting moment. "I know."

The words stopped Jim in his tracks.

Apache gave the rabbits a slight turn. "In a few days we will go home." His farseeing eyes turned southwest, as they had so often. His perfectly modeled hand indicated the stream. "Soon we cannot find water. The deer have gone elsewhere. We have used the rabbits. We must go while there is still time."

"Time! Who cares about time?" Why did an icy finger seem to count Jim's ribs? He met his foe's eyes squarely. "I haven't forgotten why you dragged me here, Apache."

His meaning was clear. Apache's smile twisted into contempt. "If you ever knew." He threw his ax across the small clearing, until it imbedded itself in a nearby cottonwood, and stalked off.

Jim glared, his joy melting into the old hatred. So he was cured. It didn't change the ruthless way Apache had kidnapped him or that Mescal planned it. He'd been too tough for them.

A twinge of shame sent red into his face, clean-shaven now with materials Apache had fetched along. Memory of long nights with the red man near forced him to admit that without Apache — he shut that door tight. Apache felt he had a debt to Mescal. What would she say when he rode back in, instead of Apache reporting his death? He closed his eyes and pictured her shock. It soothed his anger. When he got through telling Jon of the little plot, Mescal would pay for her treachery, and so would Apache. His teeth flashed white in anticipation, giving him the look of a snarling wolf.

The next day Apache busied himself with packing. Jim roused from his excitement and helped. Their supplies were dangerously low and as Apache had said, game scarce. They were leaving none too soon.

"Where did the deer go?" Jim raised his eyes to the end of the valley.

Apache shook his head. "They have ways." His deft fingers never missed a stroke of their work. "They are not helpless — like white men."

Jim was silenced, but the roar of vengeance in his head rivaled the diminished roar of the waterfall exit to the valley. He had decided to wait until he was closer to home to jump Apache. It was doubtful if he could get out of this hellhole without guidance. "I won't kill him," he whispered into Shalimar's mane. "But I'll make him crawl. Maybe I'll wait until we get home, so Mescal can see it."

At last they started: Jim first, the two lightly burdened burros, Apache last, on King. Jim turned back for a final glance. His face contorted. The sunlit valley had been the scene of agony and ecstasy, despair and hope. A faint haze from their last campfire still rose and hovered in the still air, the mute evidence dying before his eyes. It was as untrodden as when they came, except for lack of game. In the bowels of the earth it had been and would be an undisturbed pocket, hidden from people by its protecting cascade of water.

"Come."

Apache's reminder set Jim's face the other way. He slowly entered the cave that gave entrance to the valley, riding its dark depths this time in full knowledge, not half dead to his surroundings. Shalimar daintily picked his way and gained access to the crumbling ledge outside the waterfall. The burros started across, then hesitated.

"Keep them moving!" Apache ordered. "Tighten that lead line!"

All Jim's resentment bubbled into a great sore. He jerked the line. Shalimar jumped ahead. An instant later the line was torn from Jim's palm with a force that left it raw and bleeding. He whipped around. Froze.

"Look out!" he shrieked as a boulder bounded from somewhere above.

Apache pushed King forward, but the second burro brayed in fear and backed into the gray. King reared just as Apache reached for the lead line and crashed into the burro. Off balance, Apache grabbed for the reins. He was too late. King snorted and scrambled out of the pounding boulder's way, but not before the red giant neatly swept Apache from the saddle into a huddled heap next to the waterfall.

Jim had all he could do to quiet the animals. He managed to get them up the trail a hundred yards and find a place wide enough to tie them. Then he slipped and slid back to Apache, leaping the missing spot in the path in a jump that left him breathless.

Frantically, he clawed aside smaller rocks, straining to lift the boulder. He uncovered Apache's face. There was pain in the dark eyes, but he was alive.

A thrill of something indescribable sprayed through Jim, and he redoubled his efforts.

It was no use.

"Go, white man." Apache's voice rang weirdly in Jim's ears. "You have your wish. Apache is buried."

Jim recoiled. He could feel the blood receding from his face as he stared at the pinned-down victim, helpless but unbowed.

"Go." Apache's voice was stronger now. Was it a final spurt of energy before death? "Follow the water. Turn right at all major canyon crossings. There is enough food. Kill the burros, if you must. Use the water sparingly." He licked his lips. "Tell Mescal —" He heaved upwards and fell back.

It was the hour he had dreamed of, the

chance he had prayed for. To make Apache suffer the way he had suffered! He would die, but a horrible death. Buzzards would come while he lived and pick out his eyes. If he was fortunate, he'd remain unconscious. If not. . . . Jim's heart leaped. He had his revenge. All he had to do was get on Shalimar and go.

He sprang to his feet, face dark with passion. "Die, redskin!"

Apache's eyelids fluttered but remained closed.

Jim gave an exultant yell, reminiscent of his Indian-fighting days. One more dead Indian for the record. He backed away, keeping his eyes on his enemy, feeling his way across the broken trail, poising himself for the leap that would separate them forever.

Apache opened his eyes. The old contemptuous smile settled across his face. "Good-bye, white man." His eyes closed. The one free hand fell limply to the rocks and hung against them, blood making dark paths down the fingers and dripping into the water.

For an eternity Jim hovered on the edge of two worlds. Suspended in time, unable to move, he fought — and lost. Unwilling steps carried him back to the fallen man.

Even more reluctant steps brought Shalimar as close as he could get the big horse to Apache. Five, ten, thirty minutes he struggled to get a rope from the saddle horn around the boulder, failing each try, until, "Now!"

Shalimar sprang. Jim tugged. Apache lay free, bloodstained and broken.

In spite of his newfound strength, it was no easy task to carry Apache even to a spot where he could be lifted to Shalimar's back. It was even harder getting Shalimar to jump the gap, but at last Jim had Apache hoisted aboard the black. He led Shalimar through the waterfall and cave, hating the very thing he was doing, cursing himself for a fool.

Apache was limp, apparently lifeless. Yet Jim found a faint heartbeat and rejoiced. He stripped the Indian, checked him from raven hair to calloused soles. "Broken ribs, maybe three. Broken ankle. Smashed foot." He enumerated as he worked. "If an end of a rib or splinter doesn't hit the lung, he might make it." His laugh was gall. But his hands were gentle as he bound the ribs tightly, heated water and bathed the foot and tugged the broken ankle until it snapped back into place. Last, he made crude splints from sticks of cottonwood limbs. It was all he could do.

"More than I should do," he said harshly.

Apache moaned once but mercifully remained unconscious. It wasn't until Jim sank back on his heels that he felt himself watched and saw Apache's eyes were open.

"Now it's my turn." Jim deliberately looked deep into the black pits of pain. He held out a cup with a mixture of the herbs he'd found in Apache's saddlebags.

Apache grimaced, swallowed, and reclosed his eyes. It was the beginning of a curiously reversed but well-known time period. Jim used the same tactics on Apache that had been used on him.

The third day Apache motioned Jim to listen. "You must go." The urgency in his command was underlined by his fever-bright eyes.

"Not until you can travel." It was a relief to say it aloud, the decision that had cost Jim sleepless, troubled nights.

"Fool!"

Jim shrank from the blaze in Apache's face. "You can't call me anything I haven't already called myself." He thrust his hard-set jaw nearer. "Don't ask me why I didn't just ride off. I don't know."

Apache brushed it off as unimportant. "If you don't go now, you will die here."

A chill tickled Jim's spine.

"The stream will disappear. Even though we can get water from the waterfall, much of our way there will be none. It is already late July. No man, even a red man, can live through August here if the rains do not come. We will scorch like lizards in a frying pan."

"Then we'll scorch together. Remember what you said?" Jim's intensity made claws of his curled fingers. "I told you I'd see you in hell. You answered I'd be there with you. Now that's just where we are — together. Either we both get out, or we die here — together."

Apache's eyes turned to molten metal, reflecting the burning sun. "I was never going to tell you. You didn't deserve it!" Some of the color drained from beneath his skin, until for the first time, Jim saw resemblance to the way his white father must have looked. "Mescal sent me here with you, not to see you die, but to live."

"That's a cheap, conniving trick to get me to leave." But Jim's twisted lips had gone white.

"I do not lie, white man," Apache's sonorous tones rolled into the quiet valley. "She said, 'Bring him back well — for me.'"

82

There was no mistaking the truth.

Jim reeled, caught in a fury of crashing walls of hatred, understanding, and regret. With an inarticulate cry, he turned and ran as if pursued by a hundred howling wolves.

Hours later, he returned. Something in his face warned Apache not to reopen the subject. Jim had faced his crossroads and chosen. Even for the love Mescal had for him — and there was no denying it when Apache spoke as he had — Jim could not, would not leave. He had been forced to admit his entire stance about the fallen Indian had been wrong. Every indignity he had suffered had not been Indian revenge, but the necessary ingredients of saving his life! At last he knew what Apache had said when he flung out, "If you ever knew." Beyond the bitterness of past months something was born inside the oldest Son of Thunder, and that was gratitude for the half-breed who had done what he must.

Jim silently prepared a small meal, conscious of their rapidly dwindling supplies. It would be days and weeks before Apache could travel. Lips thinned with concentration, he apportioned the food then eyed the two burros. As Apache had said, if worst came to worst. . . .

Days later Jim stood on a small mound near their campsite, straining his eyes toward a small white cloud sailing overhead, fervently wishing it would join forces with the few other clouds. The earth had grown parched. The sun set nights in hazy, menacing purple streaks of heat. The little stream had vanished before the sun's demanding rays. For the past three days Jim had carried water from the waterfall.

A soft footstep behind him announced Apache's presence. He had hobbled the short distance, with the aid of a cottonwood limb. "Jim," he didn't seem to notice Jim's involuntary start. It was always "white man," or "Son of Thunder." Apache lifted one hand. "Tomorrow you go. If you wait longer, we will be trapped here until the fall rains. If they do not come," his shrug eloquently completed the sentence.

"You aren't ready to ride."

"No."

It hung in the air between them, until Jim roughly said, "I told you we'd go or stay together."

Apache searched the face grown strong and hard, then said, "You would give up home, love, life, for a stinking redskin?"

"No. For a — friend." For the first time, Jim held out his hand.

Apache stared at it, more emotion in his face than Jim had ever seen before, but he did not take Jim's hand.

"Jon asked once what the greatest thing was a man could do for another. I said save his life. He asked what if that meant dying in another man's place, and I told him —" Memory choked off the words for a second. "I said not many men would do that." Jim turned squarely toward Apache. Blue eyes clashed with brown. "You took a chance on that. You knew I'd kill you if I could get a chance." His face worked. "Still you brought me here — and I'm alive."

Apache gripped his hand. "It was for Mescal." His look never wavered.

"I know. But I still owe you." He forced a hoarse laugh and turned toward camp. "The best way you can help me is to get well so we can both go home."

That night Jim dropped into uneasy, troubled sleep. He awakened to find it was still dark, except for the light of the uncaring white stars. What had he heard? Tuned to catch Apache's movements when he lay helpless, now Jim could feel more than hear some foreign sound.

He slowly turned his head.

Apache was creeping toward him, catlike in the dimness.

Jim lay inert, the old dread crawling through his pores. *What is the Indian doing?* His fingers felt for the butt of his gun even while he remembered he'd tossed it aside earlier.

Intent on his task, Apache didn't notice when Jim cautiously changed position so he could observe better. The starshine glinted on a gun barrel. Through the clear night air came a faint whisper, "Good-bye, white man."

Nausea rose in Jim at the treachery of the bronzed man who had taken his hand only hours earlier. He stared through the gloom at the impassive face that turned toward him. Indescribable sadness etched deep hollows in a face gone grotesque.

A flash of understanding brought Jim to his feet even as Apache turned the gun to his own head. The shot went wild, lost in the clusters of stars above. Jim's launching of his body, like a bullet, had struck the gun in time.

Apache fought, to no avail. His former superb strength had been drained. Minutes later he lay panting on his tarp, with Jim astride his midriff. "Why did you stop me?" The terrible accusation echoed in the valley. "You could have saved yourself." His struggles ceased, but his face shone, contorted in the pale light of the watching stars.

"We stay together." Jim shook his fist in Apache's face. The gun lay in the red dust. "Do you think I'll go back and tell Jon and Mescal you killed yourself to save my hide?"

Apache winced, and Jim pressed his point. "I swear to you that if you try again and succeed, I'll stay here with your body until both of us are buzzard bait!" He climbed off Apache and towered above him. "Before Almighty God, that is my vow to you."

Apache lay motionless, eyes glittering. Then he rolled over, awkwardly got to his feet, and held out his hand.

Day after weary day succeeded one another. After that one night, neither mentioned leaving. Apache healed, was ready to ride — but too late. The streams needed for them to make the arduous journey were bound to be dry. Everything depended on if it rained, or when. They killed one burro and choked down the tough meat. Then the second. When it was gone, their supplies had dwindled to a little flour and salt. Apache fried "dough gobs" on rocks heated in the fire, tasteless pieces of bread made from flour and water with salt.

When the flour ran out, Apache came into his own. Jim tramped the valley, vainly watching for anything that moved. He would even have killed and eaten a buzzard, but ironically, none came. He returned to camp empty-handed, to find Apache roasting small pieces of meat on pronged sticks over the fire.

"Eat." Apache held out a morsel.

Jim obeyed, chewed the rather tough meat but glad to get something inside his always-hungry stomach. "What is it?"

"Lizard."

The meat came back up. Jim choked. But at the look in Apache's eyes, he forced himself to swallow, take more. "If anyone'd ever told me I'd eat lizard I'd have —" He shook his head.

"Men will do what they must to survive." Apache chewed thoughtfully. He was thin to the point of emaciation, as was Jim. "At least some men." He paused and Jim held his breath. In the comradeship of necessity Apache had begun to talk more, open up. Was it because there was little chance they would ever escape their red-walled prison?

"I am like the mule, Jim. Not horse. Not ass. A breed between, who belongs nowhere. White men curse and hate me.

Red men despise me. I am nothing."

Jim searched for words. None came. There were no words to meet the exquisite suffering.

"My mother was beautiful, but an Indian. My father was respected, until he married her. Better for me if I had died in the massacre." Apache raised a hand to still Jim's protest. "Your brother preaches a God who loves all. If it is true, then why must I walk alone? I can never marry an Indian. I am too much white. I can never marry a white woman. The ones who would have me are as rotting leaves." His gloomy face darkened a shade. "I will die, be buried in a nameless grave, forgotten. There will be no son to carry on my name. I cannot bring another into this world to bear what I suffer. One day the Apache will be gone forever, tamed and herded by the white man, the same way other tribes have gone.

"But one day the Apache will be free. And that is the day we are all dead." He sprang to his feet and paced beside the fire. "The white man will build houses and schools. He will destroy the game and despoil the streams. Then he will remember the Apache — and know he has killed part of this land."

Jim sat stunned, blood racing through his veins. The truth of what Apache had said hit him like a cannonball. He watched the tall, haggard figure limp away into the cave entrance and was aware of cataclysmic revelations he could never let Apache know he had been given.

Apache loved Mescal. His eyes, constantly turned toward the southwest, betrayed him to the man who had been forced to spend weeks and months in this dying place with him. It was not the love Jim found had grown within his own heart since that day he learned she cared — a love that looked forward to possession, sharing, and happiness. Apache's love transcended human feelings. His greatest joy would be serving her, never letting her know he loved, and at last dying to save for her the unworthy, sniveling coward who had crawled home to die.

Jim set his jaw, watching the same southwestward direction Apache sought, seeing beyond canyons and red rocks, valleys and mountaintops and plateaus to the Triple S basking in the summer sunlight. Was Mescal even at this moment facing northeast, keeping her secret, praying and hoping and passionately longing to see them return? She would know they were long overdue. Did she watch every cloud, cursing it when it lazily drifted on, willing it to spill its blessed contents on the earth?

"If it doesn't rain soon, it will be too late." Apache's voice roused Jim. He glanced away to keep from betraying knowledge of Apache's carefully hidden secret. "What date is it?"

"Somewhere near the first of September." Apache's grim voice did little to reassure. "Now all we can do is wait. . . ."

PART II
Jon

5

Jon Sutherland stumbled down the attic stairs, self-reproach in every step. How could he have slept when Jim needed him so much? It had seemed like good sense when Mescal ordered him to get some rest after Jim's spell subsided, and he dropped into unconsciousness, but the sun streaming in through his window this morning accused Jon. The long strain must have been too much even for his toughened body — he'd gone out like stars before a sullen sky.

The room to Jim's door was closed when Jon got to it. He put one hand on the knob, intending to slip in as he had so many times before while his twin lay sleeping. It turned under his hand, then opened wide. Mescal stood in the doorway, a strange exalted look on her face. Jon could see rumpled sheets and blankets on the bed in back of her. "Why, what on earth — ?" He stared. "Where's Jim?" Fear seized him. Had last night's spasms been the last? He grabbed Mescal's shoulders, shook her roughly. "He isn't. . . ."

"No." It hung in the air.

"Then where is he?" Jon demanded.

"Gone."

Jon's fingers tightened. He saw Mescal wince and hastily let her go. "I'm sorry, Mescal. It's just that I don't understand. Where has he gone and how?"

Something flickered in her eyes, steadied. A tiny pulse beat in her throat. Her arms hung motionless at her sides. "Apache took him away."

Blood leaped to Jon's brain. "Apache dared?" Jon whirled, his high-heeled boots clicking on the board floor. "And all this time we thought he was our friend!" Jon couldn't remember ever having been so enraged. "How much of a head start do they have?" He snatched his sombrero from the rack near the door and ran to the porch.

"Wait!"

Jon heard the sound of her moccasined feet behind him and turned back. "Don't try to stop me. Tell Dad and Mother I'll bring him back, and as for that Judas Indian —"

"Stop it!" Mescal caught his shirtfront in great handfuls, pulling him toward her. "Apache isn't going to harm him. Jim has gone away for our sake, so we won't have to see him die. Can't you understand? Would you stay here and see us suffer, if it were you?"

His anger fled, replaced with illumination. "You mean Jim came all the way home to be with his family and now has turned around and gone off somewhere with an Apache to die?" He shook his head to clear the mist swimming in his brain. "It doesn't make sense."

Golden motes struggled to overcome misery in her dark eyes. "It's killing your folks and you, seeing Jim as he is."

"And you, Mescal?"

She sagged, and he was sorry he'd added the question. He put both arms around her, something he hadn't done since she'd grown up. He could feel the hard beating of her heart, but he had to lean close to catch her whisper, "And me." His hold tightened. Somehow he had always known it was Jim, even in the years and years his brother had been gone. Life was funny. It would be logical for Mescal to turn to the brother who had stayed home. Instead her heart had gone with the prodigal.

"Well! Never thought I'd catch you two spoonin' right outside Jim's window." Matthew Sutherland's hearty voice separated them, and his big grin spread across his face. "What's Jim to say about this?"

"Jim's gone. Gone somewhere with Apache to die in peace," Jon hastily added, when the smile faded in his father's eyes.

"No more than I'd have expected. Mother will take it hard, but I don't know but what that's best." Matthew smoothed the heavy gray forelock back out of his eyes. "The Indian'll take good care of Jim and let us know after it's over." He wheeled and strode into the house. "I'll tell Mother." A low cry a few minutes later split the silence, and Jon bolted to the corral. Dad could care for Mother better than he could until he overcame his own heartache.

Weeks later, Jon reined in the black he'd taken for his special horse since Apache and Jim rode away on King and Shalimar. "You're a grand horse, Dark Star," he told the stallion. "It isn't your fault you aren't gray and fleet as the wind." Regret filled him. "I never even got to tell him good-bye." But he knew he wasn't talking about the animal. Doubts assailed him. Why hadn't Apache returned? In the shape Jim was in, he couldn't have lasted. If something had gone wrong, and Apache'd been attacked, somehow he would have set King and Shalimar free. Jon would bet his life on it.

It had been such a strange summer: first Jim's homecoming, then his leaving. Sometimes Jon caught a look in Mescal's eyes that made him wonder. Was she hiding something? If so, what? She never lied. Still she acted strange. Dozens of times he had caught her looking north and east. Once he said, "Did they go that way?"

"Yes."

He prodded no more. Mescal had never been heavy, but she thinned to aspenlike straightness as summer laid its scorching blanket over the rim. Day after day they waited for rain, and none came. Stillness settled over the family, each waiting, watching, perhaps praying for Apache's return. "Waiting kills," Dad remarked once, out of Mother's hearing. "She'll feel better once she knows it's over."

Jon caught sight of Mescal's face as she turned and slipped away into the woods. Suspicion crystallized. Mescal knew something the rest of them did not. He followed her, but she outdistanced him, and when she came back hours later, avoided him.

Now Dark Star whinnied and tossed his head for attention. Jon sighed. Dad was right — the waiting was killing them all.

He slid from the saddle and tossed Dark Star's reins over his head. All the Triple S horses were trained to stand that way. A rocky promontory ahead lured him, and Jon dropped to the outcropping. What was he to do about his own life? Deep inside was the desire to become a minister, to bring hope and healing to those around him. Yet how could he leave now? He shook his head. His plans and dreams had to wait.

What if Apache never came back? Why hadn't he followed them that morning long ago, insisted he be part of Jim's death, the same way he'd been part of his life? Some minister he would make, when he couldn't even reach his own twin!

Dark Star nickered, and Jon raised his head. Fifty feet away, Mescal, on Patches, stood gravely surveying him. Girl and pinto seemed of one piece in the green surroundings. Jon had been so engrossed he hadn't heard them coming. He stood and started toward them.

"I'll come to you." Mescal expertly dismounted. The boy's pants she wore for riding, over the protest of Mrs. Sutherland, didn't hamper her the way the girl's long skirts did. She left Patches to graze near Dark Star and glided to Jon's perch. Disquiet rested in her eyes, and Jon could feel tension in the slim body, when they seated themselves again.

"What were you thinking? You looked so grim when we rode up." Mescal sifted a handful of pine needles and let the dirt slide through.

"I was wishing I'd followed Jim."

She started. A deep flush faded into alarming whiteness, but she only said, "It wouldn't have done any good."

Suddenly Jon could stand it no more. "Mescal," he measured every line of her face and nervous hands. "You know more than you're telling, and I'm going to find out what it is."

Instantly she was on guard. It showed in the way she leaned back from him and in the mocking light that rose to change her face completely. "Oh? And just what is it I'm supposed to be hiding? What guilty secret are you accusing me of?" Her quickly assumed mask wasn't good enough to cover the flash of fright in her eyes, just before she glanced away.

"If I knew, I wouldn't have to ask, would I? You've been keeping out of my way ever since Jim and Apache disappeared. This is the first time we've been alone together." He dropped a hard hand over her small, shapely brown one on the ground between them. "Mescal, dear, what's come between us? Even if you love Jim, I'm your brother who loves you."

His tenderness hit a soft spot. He knew it reached the mark through the quick clutching of his hand by her strong fingers. A rock crystal sparkled in her dark lashes, and she shook her head to get rid of it. "It's just the waiting. If you only knew how hard it is!"

"Don't you think I do?" Gruffness replaced Jon's understanding. Anger at his own helplessness washed through him again and again. "There should have been more I could do. Instead, Jim went off into the desert or mountains or valleys somewhere. I can almost hear his voice calling me to come, the way he called me to follow his lead all the time we were growing up. But I don't even know where to start! Mescal, tell me where they went. I have to find my brother's grave and at least mark it. I can't stand thinking he's lying in an unmarked hole under a sand dune or a pile of rocks." He'd never meant it to pour out like that. Once started, the dam of anguish smashed before his tongue could stop it.

Mescal turned to stone. Each feature seemed chiseled by the harsh land in which they lived, where danger lurked beneath even the most beautiful day.

"Tell me, Mescal. Where is my brother's body?"

For a long moment she didn't answer. At last she turned to him. Her eyes were hollow as the brassy sun already poured out on them. "I don't know."

He recoiled. "But you said Apache took him, that they'd gone north and east." He was almost incoherent from the desolation in her confession.

"It's all true. Apache took him. I told him to."

For an instant Jon thought the hot breeze that had whipped by played tricks on his ears. He closed his eyes and reopened them. No, it wasn't a dream. He was still on the rocky promontory. He could see every direction, most of all the direction she'd said Apache and Jim had gone.

Mescal fixed her eyes on a distant tree and said in a monotone voice, "Apache said, if he could take Jim away, there was one chance in a thousand he could save his life."

Jon leaped to his feet, blood hot in his face. "You believed him?"

"What choice was there? We all knew he was dying. Even your father said it was better this way." Her lips set in a stubborn line. "I did what I thought was right. I still think it was, even now that —"

"That what?" he thundered. "Do you realize what you've done? You sent my brother into the wilderness to die with no one but an Indian. You knew how he felt about them. How did you persuade Jim to go?"

Her drooping head was answer enough. Jon clenched his hands until the nails broke the skin of his tough palms. "You didn't persuade him. You ordered Apache to abduct him, didn't you?"

"Yes!" Her cry rang from rock to rock, bounced off into a million shattered echoes, the way Jon's faith in her broke.

"Why? Why did you do such a terrible thing?" Jon panted for breath after the blow. "You knew how we all loved him. Yet you chose to —" he strangled on the words. "Is this the way you repay all our family has done for you?" He knew the taunt was caustic and rejoiced.

"I'm part of this family." Her eyes glowed like twin coals. "I wasn't born into it — Mother and Dad chose me to be in it. You talk about love — there are many kinds of love. Mine was strong enough to take a chance, that's all." She stood her ground, magnificent in her denunciation. "You smothered him. You would never have agreed to let him have that one long chance. I did."

The quivering aspens grew still at her defiance. The world held its breath. Even the cloud lazily strolling by paused.

She wasn't finished. "Don't you know I've asked myself the same questions a million times in the past few weeks? Don't you know that along with the sorrow we all share I've had to fight guilt? But in spite of the way it has turned out, if I had the choice to make again, this very minute, I'd do the exact same thing! I believe in fighting for life, not placidly accepting that the chips are down and hanging on to a rotten hand. At least I had the courage to give him that one chance."

Jon's brain reeled the way a small rock broke loose and merrily skipped down the cliff. "Then since Apache hasn't come back — Jim could still be alive." A sentence blazed in red-hot letters. "What do you mean, in spite of the way it's turned out?" Incredible hope turned to blackness.

Every ounce of fight drained from the girl before him, leaving her stark and spiritless. "If Apache had been able to make Jim live, they would have been back."

"Maybe not." Once she had instilled the possibility of life, Jon refused to let it die. "Maybe it took longer than Apache expected. Maybe they will ride in any day!" He spun around, lifted both hands to the sky. "As you said, Apache hasn't come back. Neither have Shalimar nor King. If Jim were dead, one of the three should have come!"

"Not from where they were going."

Mescal's words plowed into him like bullets. Jon could feel hope slipping, in spite of his frantic clutch at straws. "Where was it?"

"The Utah brakes."

"Then I'll go after them!" Jon could feel his heart glow. He dropped to one knee beside Mescal. "I'll find them, if it's the last thing I do on this earth."

"You can't. Even Apache wasn't sure he could find the place he wanted. His grandfather told him of a strange country through the Paria Plateau. There's a hidden valley, back of a waterfall. But if Apache didn't find it, he'd go somewhere else." Her dark head swung back and forth. Defeat slouched her shoulders. "There's been no rain. Even if they got there, and Jim got well, they couldn't recross the desert and get home."

A death knell drummed in Jon's ears. Everything she said was true. The hot summer had taken its toll even here. What would it be in a place such as she'd described?

"Do you think I should tell Dad and Mother the whole truth? I never lied. I just held back part of what really happened." Mescal's searching eyes insisted on an answer.

Jon felt weak from the rainbow of emotions he'd experienced: rage, relief, hope, despair, and gradual acceptance. He sank back to the ground beside her. Jim really was dead. There could be no doubt about it. Apache probably was, too. Shalimar and King might turn up on someone's ranch someday, if they got out of the box canyon.

"I think it would just make more hurt," he said carefully.

"You blame me, don't you?"

She looked so small, so defenseless, Jon was reminded of her at six, when she'd been so sick they thought they would lose her. Compassion swept through his body. What a burden she had carried! "No, Mescal, I don't blame you now. You did what you had to, what I couldn't have done. It isn't your fault the odds were too great. If Jim were here, I think he'd thank you for being willing to at least let him stay in the game."

Her enormous eyes devoured him. She gasped, then slipped to her feet, called Patches, and barely touching the stirrup, mounted. "I'll see you back at the house." Before he could reply she was gone.

It was just as well, Jon thought. He'd lived a lifetime in the past hour. The sun was still as brassy; the leaves of the aspens had quivered back to life; the curious cloud had gone on about its business, yet everything had changed. Jon threw himself full-length on the needle-strewn ground. "I suppose I'm still in a shocked state," he told Dark Star, who had come closer. "Part of me is dead. Jim's gone, for keeps. Even when he was fighting Indians, I always knew he would come back. I always felt, if anything happened to him, I'd know it, because I was part of him.

"I still don't feel he can be gone, even though I know he has to be. There was one chance in a thousand, and Mescal was willing to try it. Well, there's maybe one chance in a million that Jim and Apache are holed up somewhere, waiting for the rains. Why not believe it until summer's over and fall comes? Time enough then to say good-bye." He lightly vaulted to Dark

Star's back and followed the trail Patches and Mescal had taken toward the ranch.

In the next few weeks, Jon observed Mescal closely. Her confession had freed her. Some of her rosy hue returned to chase the dead white from her face. She smiled more often — and he never saw her look toward the northeast. It was as if, in accepting the worst, healing had begun.

Not so for Jon. Jim's laughing face peered at him from every small pond of water, every deep glade, each place they'd roamed together. Sometimes it was the way Jim had been at six or eight, other times twelve or sixteen — never the emaciated, drawn countenance of the dying man.

At first Jon started whenever his twin's image rose to his mind. Then he shrugged. With Jim on his brain so much of the time, it was natural. Besides, there was plenty to do. Ranch chores were never done, and this summer they cried for his attention. He took a morbid joy in branding cattle, herding horses, even working in the vegetable garden. While his parents never lost the shadows in their eyes, Jon's natural buoyancy restored some of the happy home they'd known.

"Now it's *you* who looks northeast."

Mescal slipped up behind Jon one evening when silver streaked skies and clear lemon clouds trimmed with old rose sent flattering glances at the coquetting aspens.

"Habit, I guess." Jon had decided not to let Mescal know a lingering hope filled his heart. Maybe it was merely stubbornness, yet it remained with him.

"It's too late, you know."

"Too late for what?" Matthew Sutherland stepped out. "You two fighting again? Seems as if you'd make up and settle down. Mother and I'd be mighty proud if Mescal Ames became Mescal Sutherland."

"So would Jon Sutherland," Jon told his father wryly after Mescal fled, her face the color of the sky.

"Is it the memory of Jim standing between you?"

"Partly. There are other things." Jon bit his tongue. It wasn't the time to tell how he wanted to be a minister and that even if Mescal loved him, instead of his twin, it would be a hard life for her. He watched the sky redden even more, then purple into dusk. "Another hot day tomorrow."

"Sure will be." His father heaved himself up from the step. "Reckon it's bedtime soon. Busy days." His face shadowed before he went back inside. "Too bad things didn't work out different. We could have used Jim. Now it's just the Double S."

"Don't ever change it!" Jon's voice rang in the gloom following the spectacular sunset. He laughed to cover the sharp command. "Besides, Mescal makes it Triple S, doesn't she?" He felt the sharp scrutiny in watching gray eyes before his father said, "I hope so, son," and left him alone on the porch.

August died, and September was born. Even Jon's determination shook. The parched land cried for water. His parched heart cried for reassurance. Mescal was the only one he could talk to, and he wouldn't admit to her how he clung to an impossible idea. Yet never did he take time from his work to rest without facing northeast with a prayer in his heart. Not a formal pleading to an Unseen Power, but an unspoken "please, if there's any hope" sustained him through the long, hard days and nights. More than once he stopped what he was doing and listened. But the sound that whispered "Jon" in his ears was merely the chatter of squirrels or a rustling in the grass or the cry of a hawk. He knew Mescal was concerned about him, and even as she'd avoided him earlier that summer, now he tried to keep away from her.

He did not succeed. She caught him at dawn, saddling up for another hard day. "You've got to stop working this hard," she scolded. Her simple dress showed she was doing inside work, probably helping can the hundreds of quarts of fruits and vegetables and meat they'd need for the winter. The rolled-up sleeves showed the line where tanned hands met smooth, white arms.

"Work never killed anyone." He hadn't meant to sound so abrupt, but he didn't want to talk to her just then. He'd awakened from a dream in which Jim called over and over, but Jon couldn't get his legs to move to go help him.

"I wish I'd never told you the whole truth," she blazed, dark eyes glaring at him. "Ever since then, you've hoped for a miracle."

"Who's to say there won't be one?" He set his lips firmly and led Dark Star away from the house.

"Just because you want to be a minister, you don't have to be an ostrich. It's nearly the end of September. Do you really think, after all these months, they could be alive?" Scorn lashed him, and Mescal rushed on. "Oh, yes, I know what you want. You want Jim to come back and everyone to live happily ever after, the way it is in fairy tales." Some of the rage left her face, and she leaned toward him, sympathy in her eyes. "Jon, it just isn't going to happen that way."

The truth of what she said drove the last bit of hope from Jon. He had to strike out, hurt as he was hurt. "Who do you think you are, God? First you play the all-wise one and arrange all this. Now you insist on destroying even my sanity. Why don't you just leave me alone?" He regretted it the minute the words were out.

Her face turned deathly pale. "I'll never forgive you for that, Jon Sutherland. Never!"

"Mescal, I'm sorry."

"Sorry's too late. I know now you never did accept what I did, even though you said you understood." Her total control frightened him. "Just when I was beginning to think —" her sentence died. She left him without another word.

"Come back, Mescal." He started for her, but she reached the house before he could gain on her swift stride.

Reality had caught up with him. Not only must he acknowledge his clinging to an unbelievable possibility was stupid, now he had treated Mescal abominably. She wouldn't forgive, either, not after the way he had turned on her as a mistreated cur turns on his cruel master. Any hope of her caring for him, when Jim didn't return, was gone, killed by his own hand. He'd be lucky if she spoke to him, other than enough to keep the folks from knowing the bitter chasm between them.

September ended. At last the rains came, healing, drenching. Then came the first frost. Jon could feel it in the air when he wearily dragged in from riding fences one night. He was cold not only outside but inside. The frosty range would be nothing compared with the frost between him and Mescal. If only he could go back a few weeks and hold his temper! "Sons of Thunder" was right. First Jim had followed his wild inclination; now his brother dwelled in a wasteland of misery. He had given up his plans to become a minister. The Triple S needed him, even if Mescal didn't. The Comstocks had hired away most of their hands, at better wages, and sections of ranch were being left unpatrolled. They'd lost stock, a few horses.

One night it snowed. All Jon could see was the heavy way it hung on the evergreens, not the beauty. Snow meant death, a decent burial to all the plants and flowers that died in fall. Spring and resurrection were far away. Somewhere in the blanketed country, Apache and Jim slept. But there was no sleep for Jon. Red-rimmed eyes in the little mirror, the next day, showed what night had done. Specters he thought vanquished had stood in his room, taunting, enticing. Maybe he was going mad. His mind knew things that even yet his heart would not admit.

"Mescal," he told her brusquely at breakfast, "don't ride out today. Radford Comstock's been making threats again." He didn't add he was just about ready to ride into Daybreak and put a stop to them. One more story about the sheriff's comments, and badge or not, he was going to get the beating of his life.

"I ride where I please," Mescal reminded him. Never had she been prettier than in her simple riding outfit, with flags of color flying in her smooth face.

"You'll stay in, or I'll rope you to the bedpost," he warned and saw amazement change to rebellion in her scarlet face.

"Here now, that's no way to talk to Mescal," Matthew Sutherland protested. "Jon, what's got into you? You're touchier than a wolf with a sore paw lately."

"Just see that she stays inside." Jon's

measured gaze never left the girl. "There's going to be a kidnapping around here, if you don't." He heard a step behind him and snapped shut his mouth on what he'd been going to add. No need for Mother to know Comstock's threats.

"Shucks, ain't one kidnapping around here enough?"

Jon froze. He saw his father turn white. He watched Mescal's face flame before she hurled herself ·past him at a snow-covered figure. Still he couldn't believe — until a drawling voice said, "If I'd known my own brother wasn't going to be any more excited about my coming back, Apache and I'd have stayed out a little longer."

Something burst inside him. Jon turned, swept aside a crying Mescal, and felt himself gathered into a snowy, crushing bear hug. Thin, bearded, strange, Jim Sutherland had come home.

6

Mescal was the first to come to her senses. "I have to warn Mother. She's been so frail the shock might be too much." She fled toward the kitchen area and was stopped when the older woman stepped through the doorway.

For a single instant, she put one hand to her heart. Her face blanched. Her lips moved soundlessly. Then she dropped into a pitiful heap on the floor. If Jon lived to be a hundred, he would always associate breaking crockery with this homecoming. He started forward and was brushed aside. Jim flung off his snowy, tattered coat and knelt on the floor. "Get a glass of water," he ordered the confused Mescal. "She'll be all right. See, her eyelids are beginning to quiver."

"My son, my son!" Jon couldn't stand looking into the great gulfs of spilling pools and plunged blindly through the door. He nearly upset Apache. Like Jim, the Indian had leaned to fence-rail proportions. One of the few smiles Jon had ever seen on the rich, brown face curled the thin lips and lightened somber eyes.

If his life had depended on it, Jon couldn't have spoken. He clasped Apache's worn hand in his, acknowledging what lay between them. At last he said, voice husky with both gratitude and joy, "My two brothers have come home — and I am glad."

A lightning ripple crossed Apache's face. His grip tightened until Jon felt he must cry for mercy. Then without a word he motioned to the yard behind him.

A drooping black horse and a weary but proud gray stood with reins hanging. Snow softened their images but didn't hide ribs just below the skin. Yet to Jon, the gaunt shadows of what they had once been were beautiful. He leaped from the porch. "Shalimar!" He threw his arms around the black and was rewarded with a soft nicker. Heart in throat, eyes wet, he turned to King and buried his hot face in the shaggy mane. When he could speak again, he whispered, "Thank God — for you all." He stepped back and examined the horses. "They're thin, but they'll fatten up." His anxious gaze went back to Apache. "How — no, we'll all want to hear the story, but first, let's get these horses cared for. Dad!"

Matthew Sutherland stumbled to the porch. Great drops stood unashamedly on his face and beard. His working face told everything, and wordlessly he held out a crunching hand to Jim's deliverer. Jon felt his own throat muscles tighten in response and covered by saying, "Apache, get inside and into dry clothes. Mother and Mescal will feed you. Come on, Dad, these horses need us."

The practical everydayness of Jon's reminder cleared the air of emotion but not of snowflakes. They melted on Jon's bare head, yet felt strangely warm, a benediction to the return of his twin. He and his father worked in silence, drying, cleaning, currying Shalimar and King, then giving them grain.

"Not too much at first," Matthew warned. "They'll founder."

It took a long time to get morning chores done, when every nerve and cell in Jon's body wanted to be inside. Once Mescal came out, her strange reserve gone. "They're both sleeping. It's the best thing for them. Jim wanted to tell us, but Mother said no, not until they rested. Now it would take cannon fire to awaken either of them." She adjusted the shawl over her head, to ward off the thickening snow. Her face gleamed in the half-light made by the storm. "I was wrong, Jon. There are miracles. One just rode into the Triple S." Her face pearled into wonder. "Can you forgive me?"

"Forgive *you!*" Jon was jolted into amazement. "It's the other way around. You were right, too. But we can be thankful sometimes all the knowing in the world doesn't change how things will be."

Apache woke at sunset, an unreal, red-and-gold hour when the snow stopped and the sun flung a defiant challenge to clouds gathering forces for another attack on the earth. He refused to say anything about the journey. Jon wanted to shake him but respected the Indian's right to be silent. He couldn't keep back one question, however. "Jim's really well? There will be no recurrences?"

"There will be none." Apache looked first at Jon, next at Mescal. "Your brother is well, healed by herbs and the desert and canyons." He fell silent then added, "Perhaps even by the God my people call the Great Spirit." It was the biggest concession Jon had ever heard Apache make, and before he could reply, Apache glided to Jim's room. Jon had already peeped in dozens of times. Jim lay in a stupor, exhausted by his

ordeal but sleeping naturally and deeply —
a far cry from the tormented, thrashing
nights he'd spent months earlier. There
wasn't a moan to betray what had passed.

Twenty-four hours later, the entire
family gathered in front of a roaring fire
banked with half a log that could be
pushed in as it burned. Apache sat back in
the shadows, part of the group yet aloof.
The older Sutherlands occupied hand-
made chairs away from the blaze. Jim
stretched on a couch, with Mescal and Jon
close by.

"Now, Son," Matthew prodded. "We
want the whole story."

Jon caught the way his twin angled a
look at Mescal before his blue eyes caught
fire from the flames' reflection. "*All* of it?"

Mescal's face turned scarlet, but her eyes
flashed. "Yes. All of it."

A hundred devils danced in Jim's eyes.
"All right. Remember, you asked for it. I
was cruelly snatched from my bed by a
wild Indian, thrown on a horse, forced to
ride when I was dying, cut into, starved,
forced to submit and —," his clear gaze
sought Apache, "and healed because a
grand girl and a faithful *man* wouldn't give
up on me."

"Is that true?" his mother burst out,

veined hands clenched, horror and re-joicing on her face.

"Sure." Jon knew by the careless way Jim replied that's all they'd get as to why he had disappeared. "But let me tell you what happened after that first part." He leaned forward, thin face aglow.

"I will speak first." The voice from the shadows startled them all. Apache never put himself forward. Now there was authority in the deep tones. "If your son had not stopped to save a wounded Apache, he could have been back with you weeks ago." He described the scene when they left the valley in a few words, yet Jon could see it all — the quick fear of the burro, the smashing rock, a crumpled man beside the waterfall.

"By the time I could ride, it was too late to leave what little protection we had in the valley," Apache finished.

Jim looked at him intently, and Jon realized there was more to it than Apache was telling, but Jim shook his head and cut off anything else the Indian might add by asking, "How would you like to eat lizard, Mescal? And fried desert mice? And roots and foliage?"

Disgust left her face wrinkled. "Is that what you did?"

"Sure." It was obvious Jim was enjoying himself. "You can't believe all the stuff you can eat, if you have to, at least until it runs out." His voice faded, and his eyes glazed with memories clearer to the enthralled audience than words could have been. He shrugged it off. "Anyway, when the waterfall dried to a trickle and we polished off the last of the burro meat, we were in bad shape." His face flushed, but he met their anxious looks steadily. "I wanted to butcher one of the horses."

Mescal gasped audibly. Her hands clenched in her lap. Jon could feel her disbelief. The way Jim loved horses — nothing could have told them better how desperate and crazed he had become.

"Apache said no, they were our only salvation. When we got so weak we could barely ride, he bled King, and we drank a little. Shalimar wasn't strong enough to stand it. King carries two scars." Reverence shone on his countenance, and the dying embers cast golden sparks that matched the gleams in his hair. Jon knew with sudden clarity that never again would Jim refer to the hardships of that journey.

"We'd about given it up, although Apache said we weren't quite to the end of our rope, as long as we tied a knot and held on." His voice sank to a whisper. "I got to hate the sun. It was a personal enemy, sneering its way up mornings, gloating during the day, while we lay in what shade we could find, hating to go down at night. Apache made me walk nights, for hours, at least until my strength failed. That way we could sleep days and eat our scarce meal at night.

"I loved the nights. You know how the stars are. I used to watch them and pretend they'd drip pretty soon, and I'd catch it and get rid of my thirst. It sounds loco, but things out there were crazy."

Jon could bear it no longer. "Tell us how you got out."

"It rained." The simple words rang triumphantly. "I'd been in a drugged sleep. I woke to see Apache standing facing the sky, torrents of water pouring off him. When I could believe what was happening, I went wild. I screamed and shouted and even thanked whatever power there might be for the rain. It meant life."

Jon struggled with the disappointment Jim's words "whatever power might be" brought. Even Apache had recognized the hand of God. Why not Jim?

No longer was Jim the beaten captive of the canyon. He jumped from the couch and threw his arms out to them all. "The next morning we started home. By the time we could get to the first signs of human habitation, we were all in. You think we're thin now, you should have seen us and the horses when we got to a home-steader's little place." A strange humility filled his story. "He didn't have much, but what he had he gave. We stayed there several days. He even asked us to stay on, when the frost came, but we couldn't. We were all right by taking it in easy stages. A lot of the time we walked to spare the horses." He swallowed hard, and Jon caught a quick dash of moisture in his eyes before he finished with, "Someday I'd like to go back."

"What!" his father roared. "After all that, you want to go back?"

"Yes." Jim's chin didn't budge a fraction of an inch. "It was night when we went, or else I was too sick to care. Coming home wasn't much better. Before I die, I'm going back the same way and see what I missed." Jon shuddered at the prophetic tone in his twin's voice. Why should he feel a cold wind blowing down his back, as if the door behind them had suddenly been flung open? Jim's desire might be a little morbid, but it was natural. There wasn't anything in it to bring this premonition of some future terrible event.

"So the prodigal son returned." Jim's eyes danced. "See, I remember some of the Bible stories. This was almost like that one, wasn't it? Return of the prodigal, a great feast —" He motioned toward the remains of their bounteous dinner, where Mescal and his mother had covered things and left the dishes in order to hear his story. "One big difference, though. Seems I remember the brother in that story wasn't as happy as the brother in this one." A poignant light shone from him to Jon, belying the casual way he referred to the episode.

"That's a story to tell your children and grandchildren, huh, Apache?" Matthew chuckled. But the corner where Apache had been stood empty. He'd slipped out, unnoticed, sometime during the end of Jim's story.

Jon found him in the small cabin they'd erected for him when he came to the ranch, since he preferred not to live in the bunkhouse. "Is there anything you want to tell me, Apache? Maybe something Jim forgot?"

Black eyes fixed on him. With an expressive gesture, Apache said, "Your brother knows there is one good Apache."

All the thanks Jon had wanted to express in the earlier handshake dried up. He mumbled something and left the cabin, with Apache standing at the door. A little soreness formed around his heart. Never had there been secrets that he and Jim couldn't share. Now summer days and nights and their anguish lay between Jim and Apache, a bond not to be spoken even to a brother. He felt it again when Jim came to him later that evening. "I was wrong about Apache. He's a white man all through, and I don't mean the color of his skin." Jim didn't elaborate, just yawned and told him, "Good night, Jon. Back to our old room for us and glad to be there." His smile lingered in Jon's mind, long after Jim lay sleeping in the bed across the room, the same way they'd done since childhood.

For days after their return, Jon watched Jim for lasting effects of what Mescal called "the missing months." Early snow melted and changed into a glorious late Indian summer. Thanksgiving brought extra reason for a feast. It had a dual meaning this year. Tragedy had brushed its skirts against their hearth and been vanquished. Jim laughed and teased Mescal as he'd always done. If something new and smoldering had been added to the way he watched her, only Jon noticed. He hadn't dared broach the subject with Jim. The early time after their return found Jim wild to ride, work, and hunt. He seemed obsessed with the idea of making sure there would be plenty, in case of a long winter.

Jon watched and understood. Jim had told him through clenched teeth, "I will never, as long as I live, be hungry again." His lips had curled in an ugly snarl. "No matter what I have to do, me and mine will have food."

"We always have had," Jon reminded him. "Why think we won't now?"

Some of the defiance melted. "If you'd let me go after the Comstocks, we'd have a lot more cattle. Until we take a stand, they're going to hound us."

"Things have slacked off now. Why don't you take some time off, ride into town, and see some of your old friends?"

Jim's eyes lighted. "Good idea. How about coming with me?"

Jon shook his head. "No, I'll stay home. Go on and have a good time." But after a few times Jim was gone overnight to appear loaded with presents for them all, Jon wondered if he'd done the right thing in suggesting it. "Where'd all this truck come from?" he demanded of Jim. "Not that we can't use it." He fingered a new rifle and pointed at a braided rug on the floor and pictures neatly hung on the walls.

"Got lucky at cards." Jim's grin failed to hide satisfaction.

"All this stuff?" Jon eyed him. "Must have been pretty lucky. Who have you been fleecing?"

Jim leaned his chair back on two legs, until it squawked a protest. His grin widened. "More than one way to get back what the Comstocks have stolen from us, now isn't there? You might say I'm just taking what's rightfully ours."

"Comstocks! Better not get around that outfit." Jon hesitated then plunged ahead. "You hear any more about his being after Mescal?"

Jim's eyes turned to blue metal. "Not from him, but one of these times he's going to leave off that badge, and when he does, I'll be there."

"Get that crazy notion out of your head. If you kill a sheriff, you'll hang." Cold sweat broke out on Jon's neck at the thought. He could see Jim defending Mescal's honor and being lynched by an angry mob of Comstock relatives and friends.

"Let me handle it, little brother," Jim smiled the tormenting smile he always used when he considered a subject closed. He stretched full height, a tawny cougar ready to pounce. "Speaking of Mescal, when are you and she getting hitched?"

If Jon hadn't known him so well, he'd have missed the intensity of the nonchalant question. His face burned. "Me! It's you she'll marry. If I'm a preacher by then, I can even tie the knot." His attempt at laughter sounded good even to himself.

Jim dropped his teasing. "You really think so?" He sank back to the floor with all four legs of the sturdy chair, face eager. "The whole time we were gone, it's what kept me going."

Every word thrust iron pokers into Jon's soul, red-hot, searing.

"Apache said she told him to bring me back — for her." Jim admitted, "I thought he was punishing me, but when I got to know him, I believed him. Now that I'm home, I can't see it. She's with you all the time."

"Of course she is!" Jon rose above his heavy spirit to match Jim's confidence. "Don't you know anything about girls? I'm her brother. She can be more natural around me. You used to be her brother, but once she started thinking of you in a different way, well —" He let his unfinished explanation hide what he felt.

"Yeah, you may be right." Jim scratched his head as if puzzled. "Alice Johnson used to act the same way." He grunted. "Peculiar, ain't it? If Mescal likes me so well, seems as if she'd show it."

"Maybe she's waiting to see if you plan to stay."

It was out, the thing Jon had known would come. The way Jim responded would irrevocably affect three lives. Why didn't he answer, declare his intentions? He'd done his share of work around the place since he'd gotten back, but Jon feared the restlessness in him. Sometimes there was a look of desperation on the handsome features. Maybe, once he knew Mescal cared, it would make the difference.

"I had a lot of time to think this summer," Jim said. The faraway look Jon had seen in his eyes so many times over the past weeks stole back to their hiding place. "If Mescal really loves me, the way I think I love her —"

"*Think* you love her! Don't you *know?*" Scorn brought Jon from his chair, to glare down at his brother.

"Sure, sure." In spite of his grin, Jon knew Jim meant it, at least as far as his selfishness could love. "Anyway, if she does, we'll be married, and I'll run the Triple S into the biggest ranch in the country." There was no doubt about his enthusiasm now. "We'll take out a loan and stock it and hire riders. We'll hold what's ours and fight anyone who tries to take it away." He sprang up to pace the floor. "You can have everything you want, even be a parson."

Not everything, Jon's aching heart whispered. *Not Mescal.* He forced the thought back, glad for Jim's statement. If he and Mescal could be happy, good for them. Who was he to stand in Jim's way? Yet a rebellious part of him insisted, *Must you always give up your own dreams for him? How far will you sacrifice for your brother?*

The nagging questions haunted him: in velvet-black nights, early gray dawns, slanting sunsets. It didn't make it easier when he saw how Mescal stayed with him. Finally he spit out, "You were so anxious to get Jim back. How come you're never with him?" At the storm warnings in her look, he hastily added, "Not that I don't want you with me. I love it." He tempered his voice to disinterest, aware how hard it was to cover his own feelings. She must never suspect but that he'd accepted and rejoiced over her choice of Jim.

Mescal's dusky head drooped. "I'm not sure he cares — enough."

Jon had started to protest but was stilled by that last word. She had instinctively put her fingers on the exact thing that troubled him. Did Jim care enough, or would time be forced to deal him a second excruciating blow before he changed from lighthearted boy to a responsible, mature man and mate for Mescal Ames?

Gradually Mescal drifted to Jim. He put up a winning campaign for her love. He brought her presents until she protested. He paid her compliments, and she resembled the setting sun's rays. Every day her beauty increased. Jon gloried in it, even while exquisite pain burned within. He could only be glad no one knew. Amused by Jim's pursuit of Mescal, Matthew Sutherland watched and was glad. His wife spent every spare moment making pillowcases and sheets for Mescal's wedding, "Whenever it might be," she said primly. Jim and Mescal appeared too involved with the wonder of dawning love to see Jon's inner troubles.

Only Apache knew. He had come on Jon watching Jim and Mescal starting for a ride one afternoon. She shied away, but laughed as he snatched her and put her on Shalimar. Jon tore his gaze free when Apache said, "My brother's heart is big to give up the white flower."

Jon hadn't pretended. "It isn't easy."

"No." The resonant voice echoed through the now-quiet clearing. "Love is pain. Yet the world could not continue without it. Stags fight to the death. The wild things burrow together. Even the birds must mate. But you and I, Jon Sutherland, know loneliness." He remained etched against the sky, a tragic figure, long after Jon saddled and rode away.

In one way it brought things to a head. The day Jim and Mescal announced they would be married in the spring, Jon gathered courage in both hands and broke the news. "Mother, Dad, since surprises are being given, although this is no surprise —" He glanced at the pair holding hands after their betrothal speech. "I have a surprise, too. Before you speak, let me tell you I've considered this over and over. I want to study for the ministry."

A ricochet of rifle bullets could have produced no more pandemonium than his simple statement. His mother gasped; then a pleased smile wreathed her face. His father looked stricken, clearly amazed at the news. Apache said nothing; Mescal and Jim wished him well.

"But when did this all happen?" Matthew asked helplessly, spreading calloused hands wide. "You never said a word."

Jon leaned toward his father, earnestly pleading for understanding. "Don't you see, Dad, until Jim came back I couldn't have gone? Why waste time over that? If I'd been your only son, I never would have left."

"So I gain one son and lose another." Bitterness corroded the kindly face.

Jon heard Jim's quickened breath. How would he take Dad's reaction? Desperate, wanting to be fair, Jon said, "Jim and Mescal are staying. Some day when I finish my training — a few months, maybe — I'll be back. Not to ranch, but to make better feelings in this place. Haven't you said again and again Daybreak needs a minister, someone who can offer comfort?"

"I never knew I'd have to lose a son to get one." Defeat sagged his great shoulders, but he tried to be a good loser. He rose and towered over his son, an uncertain smile on his bearded lips. "You have my blessing, Jonathan."

He hasn't called me that in years, Jon

135

thought bleakly. *He's already accepted it, although he doesn't fully approve.* "Thanks, Dad. You know, it's your own fault for stuffing Jim's and my head with Bible stories while we were growing up!"

"Lucky it only took on one of us," Jim drawled. "Don't worry, Dad, I'll be a faithful son, and we'll make the Triple S one great ranch."

"I'll help, too," Mescal promised, face alight with happiness.

"Of course you will, and glad I am for it." Matthew got back some of his heartiness. "When Preacher Sutherland comes home for a meal, we'll have something better to offer him than a chicken neck."

In the laughter Jon noticed Apache's eyes on him, and later the Indian came to his room. Jim was still with Mescal. The sound of their low laughter drifted into the twins' room. "What would you have me do?"

Jon jerked himself up from the deep study he'd gone into. "Why, whatever you choose. You've more than paid your debt."

"There are debts — and debts. Would you have me stay and care for your brother the way you would do?"

Jon faced the enigmatic man. An issue too deep for words lay between them. He must reply, must say what was right. He chose his words carefully. "I would trust my brother — and Mescal's and my parents' lives to you, even as Mescal entrusted Jim to you months ago."

A tiny movement that could have been approval flickered in the watching eyes. "Then I will stay, as long as I am needed." Apache extended his hand and gripped Jon's. In that touch, Jon knew he had transferred his twin into Apache's keeping.

7

The bittersweet winter finally melted into spring. Was it because of the coming separation that everything seemed so intense? The cold snapped trees that had stood for years, guardians of the Triple S. The wolves howled louder and closer. Jon and Jim grew accustomed to finding where a cow had been brought down by the starving predators. Sometimes they saw skulking, gray forms disappear into the woods when they got to a frozen, gnawed carcass.

The pile of household linen steadily grew. Mescal protested, "We won't need all that! We're only going to build on one large room, and heaven knows we've enough quilts and blankets and sheets to furnish a hotel!"

Abigail Sutherland quelled her. "No daughter of mine will start married life, even to my son, without spanking new things of her own."

Happiness mingled with pain when Jon heard Mescal's trill of laughter, saw her ecstatic face over the simple white wedding gown she and her mother made. It took all Jon's control to hide his own emotions. Jim hadn't been allowed to see Mescal in the dress, but Jon was privileged — and regretted it. Her dusky face radiated charm. Her tanned skin contrasted with the froth of lace at the neck, and never had her eyes been more golden. *Portrait of a woman in love,* Jon told himself bitterly, even while he forced himself to cock his head and tell her, "Not bad for a wild Indian rider who usually wears homespun."

For every mountain there was a valley. At least Jon could give profound thanks for the change in Jim. His brother's worshipful eyes never left Mescal if she was in the room or on the trail with them. He slipped back to the good comrade he'd been years ago. He and Jon rode, when the snow's crust would support them, stalked the range and trails for wolves, searched out the weak and helpless of the now-small herd.

"I can't wait for spring," Jim told Jon one snowy day. The two had just returned from feeding the horses in the barn. Jim paused on the wide porch and shook snow from his boots. "Ugh! It's cold." He rubbed mittened hands over his face until it glowed. "Dad's agreeable to getting a loan, so we'll be restocking cattle. We don't really need horses. I'd rather wait and pick up one or two extras that are worth something than get a batch of broomtails. We'll —" His voice died, and his eyes widened. "I keep forgetting you won't be here."

Jon's cold heart warmed to the genuine regret in his brother's face. "At least we will have this winter to remember." He fell silent, thinking of the long days riding, the interminable evenings watching Jim and Mescal dreaming about their future.

"Yeah." Jim's mood lightened. "Besides, it's not as if you're going away forever."

"No." But Jon knew Jim recognized as well as he did the gulf that would soon come between them. With Jim and Mescal married, Jon studying, then preaching, never again could things be the same. He'd be back for visits, but as someone foreign to their way of life, a visitor rather than one of them, except in blood and spirit. Jon could almost feel the doors closing against him, shutting him away from all those he loved most on earth.

He shrugged off the morbid thoughts and kicked off his boots. "Mother'll have a fit if we track in on her clean floor. Can't say as I blame her. Dirty snow's not the easiest thing in the world to mop up." He bent and brushed snow off his pant legs to hide the rush of feeling he couldn't seem to shake.

Christmas came and went; January trailed behind. February opened clear and relapsed into a final frenzy. March first was the date set for the wedding. Jim had ridden down all Mescal's protests that it was too soon and swept aside Jon's objections that he wouldn't be able to marry them by then. "What difference does it make? You'll be my best man." A crooked grin tilted his face, until he looked like some elf in the old fairy-tale book Mescal still kept from childhood. "And I do mean the *best* man. Mescal should have married you, you know. Not that I'd let her," he rattled on, seemingly oblivious to the strained pose Jon assumed. "From the time I came home, I —"

Jon didn't follow the rest of it. He met Mescal's startled gaze, filled with an unasked question. Never since Jim returned had either referred to Jon's earlier attitude. Now her eyes demanded the truth — and in spite of everything Jon could do, got it. Her lips formed in a little O, but Jon shook his head, furious with himself for betrayal, fiercely glad she had learned he cared. It would do no one any harm.

"Don't be stupid," he told Jim, with a wrack between his shoulder blades. "Mescal's my sister."

"We're going to name our first boy *Jonathan*."

Jon could feel his muscles tighten, his throat constrict. Mescal cut in sharply, "Don't be talking about babies when we aren't even married, Jim Sutherland! You better treat me nice, or I may up and decide not to marry you after all," but her curved lips took all the seriousness from her threat, and Jim only laughed.

A few days later, Jon was surprised when Mescal sought him out. Her troubled eyes went straight to his heart.

"What? No shadow?" he teased, but subsided before the flash of her dark eyes.

"The weather turned so nice, Jim rode to town." Mescal sighed and followed the trail with her glance as if willing him back from whatever might hold him. "He said he thought he'd drop by and see if Radford Comstock would come to our wedding."

A chill coasted down Jon's spine. "That crazy fool!" He threw down the harness he had been mending and started for the barn. "I'll go get him."

"You won't have to. I sent Apache."

Mescal came close and looked into his face. "Jon, will he ever really settle down? Or am I tying myself to a whirlwind or tumbleweed?"

Jon fought the longing to catch her close and protect her from all hurt. "I don't know." He could not and would not lie. "Sometimes I think he will. After you're married and I'm gone, he'll have the biggest responsibility of his life. It can make a man of him."

"I really love him," Mescal whispered, her voice carried by the capricious breeze tugging at her hair. "But sometimes I wish — Jon, if only he were more like you!"

"Mescal!" Jon seized the slipping reins of manhood that kept him from pleading with her to forget his brother and marry him. "Don't. . . ."

"Don't worry about Jim," an amused voice spun them around. "He's back from Daybreak in one piece with news that Radford Comstock will be happy to attend the marriage of Mescal Ames and James Sutherland." One tawny lock of hair hung over his devil-may-care face.

Had he heard what Mescal said? Jon couldn't tell. The steely glint in the wary blue gaze betrayed nothing. Jon's heart plummeted. Jim would never understand that Mescal could love one twin with all her heart yet long for assurance of a settled future.

Jim gave no sign of anything amiss, just caught Mescal, kissed her soundly, and chuckled as she ran toward the house. "Some little wife she's going to make, huh." He headed after her, whistling a few notes of "Dixie." Yet in the few days remaining before the wedding date, Jon sensed restlessness such as Jim hadn't shown since he and Mescal announced their plans to get married. Was it spring fever, anticipation of the coming event, or something deeper and akin to the wanderlust rooted inside Jim? Jon couldn't tell. Now he concentrated on forever putting aside his own longings and waiting for the wedding. He took care not to see Mescal alone, not trusting himself to get through a final interview. And always he wondered: had Jim overheard?

The night before the wedding, Jim insisted on riding into Daybreak. "Got to tell everyone I'm getting married to the greatest girl in the West," he proclaimed. They tried to talk him out of it. It didn't help.

"A man's got a right to get drunk before he gets hitched," Jim insisted.

Mescal had remained silent, but now her

144

whole body tensed to spring. "You come back drinking, and there won't be a wedding." Indignation etched her into a statue.

"Sure there will, sweetheart." Jon hated the careless way Jim tore down her objections. "You won't give up the second-best catch in Arizona, will you? Especially since the best man's your brother?" He strode off, leaving Jon and Mescal staring after him.

He didn't come back.

Apache rode in before dawn and roused Jon from an uneasy sleep.

"Where's Jim?" Jon demanded, focusing on the erect figure at the side of his bed.

"Gone."

Jon felt he was living a repeat of another scene months before, only that time it had been with Mescal. "Gone where?"

Apache's expressive face turned south and east.

"The canyon country?" Jon shook his head to clear his disbelief. "But why?" The stone serving for his heart moved and settled back in place when Apache said, "Jim told me to give you this. I started to follow, but he cursed and sent me back, then called out he was sorry and had to do it this way."

Jon took the crumpled scrap of paper and read the words. He read them again, although there was no need. They'd already burned into his brain: THE BEST MAN WINS — AGAIN.

He sank his teeth into his lip and tasted blood. "God," it was not a curse but a prayer. "How can I tell Mescal?"

"*I* will tell her." Apache drew himself to full height. "He gave me a message only for her ears." He glided through the door, and although Jon heard no footfalls, his keen ears detected a light tapping at Mescal's door. A little scrape, a muffled cry, then the patter of flying feet.

Mescal burst in, regardless of the restraining hand Apache placed on one shoulder. Her face flamed. Her dressing gown gaped to show a hint of high-necked white gown and bare feet clung to the cold floor. "That — that *brother* of yours has done it now." She glared accusingly at Jon. "Where did he get the idea I was in love with you?"

Jon stiffened under the unspoken accusation. "Not from me. I never even let him know *I* cared." His contempt matched her own. "I believe now he overheard what you said about wishing he could be more like me. Maybe he decided he didn't want to be tied down, after all."

Common sense returned with a flood.

Mescal studied her feet. Her shoulders drooped, the heavy hair almost too heavy for her slender neck. "I'm sorry, Jon." She couldn't stop her lips from trembling, Jon saw.

"What did Apache tell you?"

Jon thought of a frightened fawn when she bravely lifted her face. "He said to go ahead with the wedding — the best man had won."

An Indian tomahawk in his vitals couldn't have hurt as much. Blood gushed to Jon's head, leaving him speechless. How long had Jim known? All the time he thought he had fooled his twin, had their special knowledge of each other been working against him? How like Jim to wait until the eleventh hour to spring his trick. Had he figured Jon would marry Mescal rather than see her embarrassed? Who knew what went on inside Jim's wild head?

"I'm going after him." Jon reached for his boots. In the split seconds after Apache went to Mescal's room, he'd jerked on pants and shirt.

"No." Mescal's dead voice stopped him short. Rays of dawn stole softly in the open window and highlighted her troubled face. "He wouldn't come back. If he did, I wouldn't want him."

Jon sucked in a breath of clean, woodsy air.

"I mean it." Her shut lips showed how much, refusing to admit the pain in her eyes. "If he was so eager to hand me over, he couldn't have really cared — enough." She turned, head held proudly, and walked out the door.

"She is wrong, but she must find out for herself." Apache's sonorous words played "Taps" in Jon's spinning brain. "Jim does love her, but he knows his wildness could destroy her."

Jon sank back to his bed in despair. "Why?" he cried. "Everything was going so well for them. What will it take to make Jim into a man?" He balled his hand into a fist and smashed it against his pillow. "I thought his brush with death would do it, but it hasn't."

"Someday he will meet what life has for him. He will not be the same again," Apache prophesied. "Until then, who knows? He rode into the canyons with the Radford Comstock relations."

The fiddle string of Jon's nerves snapped. "What?" His laugh grated. "You didn't say *the Comstocks!*"

"Yes." Apache folded his buckskin-clad arms, face impassive.

"But why? If he had to leave, why join *them?*"

A shade of reluctance reached Apache's eyes. Then he quietly said, "Apaches are good listeners. A deal has been made. The Triple S is not to be harmed so long as one of its owners rides with the Comstocks."

Sheer rage threatened to unbalance Jon's reason. "That means Jim's the same as a rustler already."

"Yes. It also means his brother and family are protected."

Somewhere under the Ice Age covering over his soul, Jon felt a match strike. Lawless, untamable, mocking that he was, Jim Sutherland loved his family — and Mescal. He had done this monstrous thing for them. Jon stumbled to the window and plucked at the sheer curtain with nerveless fingers. Once he had told his brother the greatest thing on earth would be to die for someone. What about living for someone, even though it were in shame and as an outlaw? Hot lava flowed inside his eyelids, forcing its way out. There was good in Jim. Not the kind he'd hoped for, but a mistaken idea of how to save them all — by sacrificing himself. A lonely grave, this time unmarked forever, awaited Jim. He was bound to know it. Yet he'd chosen the dead-end trail over his dream of a Triple S with great herds, choice horses. Over Mescal and the son he'd never have. Jon knew his brother too well to think there would ever be another woman for him.

"I can't let him do it," Jon groaned.

"You cannot stop him. Only Apache can follow." The tall figure stood out more plainly, now the day had begun.

"Would you do that for me — for him — for Mescal?"

"I only returned to bring the messages." Apache hesitated. "What would you have me tell him?"

"To come home, where he belongs! We'll fight the Comstocks, if we have to, but in our own way." Jon could feel his own dreams die. If sacrifice had to be made, his career must go rather than the terrible thing Jim planned.

"Can you send word you do not love the white flower?"

Sickness spread through Jon, and he slumped against the window frame. "No. But I can send word it is Jim she loves and always has."

Apache moved his head slowly back and forth, inscrutable eyes never leaving Jon's. "It will not be enough, but I will try." For the second time he glided from the room, and a little later Jon saw him emerge from his cabin. Jon headed for the door, but by the time he reached the porch, Mescal had flown to Apache. She was too far away for Jon to hear her speech, but the imploring white face said it all. The poignancy of it struck iron into Jon's heart. Her wedding morning, and Mescal stood pleading with an Apache to find her bridegroom. His lips curled ironically. For one craven moment, he considered offering himself as substitute, the way Jim had suggested.

"Skunk!" he thundered to himself. Mescal had turned back toward the house, clad in her usual worn dress, tears streaking her smooth skin. In her present state she might even accept, clinging to him for strength. No. He couldn't insult her by ever speaking. Let the neighbors come. They'd brave it out, and maybe someday Jim would return.

The older Sutherlands reacted as Jon had known they would. Matthew roared; his wife cried. Jon and Mescal had agreed not to let them know where Jim had gone, just that he had "got a fool notion in his head he wasn't good enough for Mescal and rode off a spell." If Apache did get Jim back, no use folks being any wiser. Jon sent word to the invited guests the wedding was off and gave no reason why. It was none of their business. If they chose to think Mescal had cancelled it, so much the better.

The long day droned and dragged. Nature tried to compensate by sending forth her best green buds, her brightest March sun. Mescal disappeared, riding Patches. Apache had been sent away on Shalimar. At least Jim hadn't torn off on King, but had taken Dark Star. He must have known, when he rode away, he wouldn't be back.

Jon sat before the smoldering fire with his father. For the first time, Matthew looked old. The gray hair and eyes had never aged him before, but now Jon noticed how heavy the lines had grown in his face. Did he suspect more than he'd been told?

As if in answer to his question, his father raised his shaggy head. "Looks like I've lost two sons, instead of one." There was no hint of self-pity in the statement, just fact, but it couldn't hide what Jon had tried to ignore ever since Apache came in at daybreak.

"I won't be going now."

The leonine head raised. "I'm not asking you to stay. It's your life, and you've got to live it as best you see fit." Yet hope underscored every word.

Jon neatly tied the strings around the package of his dream and put it away. "I reckon if I can be as fine a man and as good an example to folks hereabouts as you've been, that'll be enough." He forced a light laugh. "Besides, any reason why a man couldn't study the Bible and learn enough to tell folks what's in it without going away?"

"I don't know why not. Best preacher I ever heard was a circuit rider back in the hills." Eagerness warred with unwillingness to give advice in the older man's face, and Jon saw what it meant.

"Then it's still the Triple S."

"I was wondering if there'd be enough Sutherlands left to keep it that way," Matthew admitted. " 'Course Mother and Mescal and me still makes it triple, but a son's special." He rose and yawned. "Now that's settled, guess I'll wander out and see how the hands are. Gave them all a day off for the wedding and didn't have the heart to order them out when it got cancelled." He surveyed Jon, and Jon caught the twinkle in his eye. "If Apache doesn't get that brother of yours home, you'd better make up to Mescal."

Jon dropped his head and didn't answer. He heard Matthew's heavy tread across the room followed by a "got back, did you,

153

Mescal?" then light breathing at his elbow. Mescal stood motionless. Her hands clasped in front of her scarlet sweater, and she waited. For what? What could he say to her? "Did you have a good ride?"

How dumb could he get! The day she'd set apart and looked forward to for weeks now shook itself once more and hibernated, and all he could ask was what kind of ride she'd had! A picture of the unused wedding gown floated and danced before his eyes, desecrated by Jim's desertion.

"What are you going to do now?" she asked. One grumbling coal flared to light her.

He didn't pretend to misunderstand. "I'm staying."

"You're giving up your dream?"

Both of them. Had he spoken aloud? No — she still waited, clear, dark eyes demanding truth. He leaned back so his face would be in shadow, away from her searching. "There are many dreams. I'll still do what I can. Once I've studied, maybe even preach in Daybreak. Even a cowpuncher preacher will be better than none."

"I wish he'd never come back."

Jon's anger was no more at her than at the echo of the wish in his own heart. He made a futile gesture and was interrupted by her passionate outcry, "I'd accepted he was gone. I'd even begun to forget and think maybe someday —" She caught her throat. "Then he came. I believed he cared. Can't you see it's better if he'd been lost in the desert? Then the voices would have stopped after a while. Now all I can see is what will happen." Her face turned chalky. "Will it be a bullet or a rope? Better if he'd died in the inferno." Her eyes glowed red, and she pressed one hand to her lips.

Jon was shocked into protest. "You love him that much?" The world stilled for her reply. Even the burning coal stopped snapping.

"Yes."

If she had declared it in fervent tones, it couldn't have been more convincing. Jon felt his face blanch to match hers. That single word killed any hope he might ever have had. "Mescal," he took her cold hands into his warm ones. "Someday, I don't know how or when, but someday I'll bring him back to you."

A drop splashed and glittered on his hand. Her fingers convulsed; her slender body went rigid. "Do you promise?"

"I promise." The vow he made was not

the one he'd dreamed of for years, but the reward was great. Mescal threw her arms around him, pressed soft lips to his in gratitude, then fled as if pursued by demons, leaving Jon shaken to the tips of his boots.

8

Waking and sleeping, Jon Sutherland waited for one thing — Apache's return. Never a frosty morning passed that he didn't scan the clearing to see if Shalimar had come in the night. Not a busy moment passed that part of his mind wasn't on his brother. Nightmares of Jim crying for help left Jon drained, thin. Everything hinged on what Apache found out.

It ended one early March afternoon. A mud-stained Shalimar and a set-faced man rode in. Mescal erupted from the house, Matthew and Abigail close behind. Jon laid aside the ax he'd been using to split great chunks of pine.

"Well?" Matthew boomed. "Did you find him?"

Jon saw the longing in his father's face. How terrible to be the father of a prodigal son! He turned his gaze to the splattered Apache. A bloody bandage bound one hand. Circles of fatigue made half-moons under the fine eyes. Jon's hopes sank.

"Did you find him?" Matthew asked again.

"Yes."

"Where?" Jon leaped to help Apache dismount and supported him to a seat on the porch.

"In hell." Apache's ghastly voice rang in the clearing.

What do you mean?" Mescal snapped out of the frozen state they'd all gone into at Apache's appearance. Her eyes burned. Jon felt his heart turn over with pity for her and for their mother.

"He's gone into the canyon country with the Comstocks. I tracked them. There's a valley hidden between canyons that only the eagles know. It's filled with cattle." Even the anger in the dark face couldn't hide pain. "Some wear the Triple-S brand."

Abigail Sutherland caught at the porch rail for a moment. Her parchment face and twitching fingers showed her agitation. "Jim has gone in with rustlers — of our own stock?"

"Why did you tell her, Apache?" Jon cried. "Why didn't you wait and tell me when I was alone?"

Apache's lips set in a straight line. "My story is not finished. I crawled near and listened. Every Triple-S steer and heifer and calf is to be driven back. In return, your son stays with the Comstock band." He closed his eyes as if too tired to continue.

"I don't understand." Abigail pressed closer to Apache. "Why has he done such a thing?"

Jon knew it could not be hidden. "Because he'd rather sacrifice himself than see Mescal unhappy."

Matthew wagged his big head. His eyes rolled. "Jim knew Mescal was happy. What changed it?" His heavy breathing set the air quivering with trouble.

"Once Mescal told me that although she loved Jim with all her heart, she wished he could be more like me." Jon knew a dark stain colored his face but kept steadily on. "I know now he overheard, decided in time she'd learn to — to care for me, if he left." He turned unseeing eyes toward the drooping Shalimar, outlined against the swaying aspens. "She never would. But Jim wouldn't see it like that. I sent Apache to tell him."

Every eye swung back to the Indian when Jon asked, "Did you see him at all? Did you give him my message?"

"I did." Apache's form straightened.

"And?" Eternity waited on the answer. Jon felt his heart skip a beat.

"He said to tell you once he rides down a trail, he doesn't ride back."

It was so like Jim, Jon could almost see the bright head toss and the mocking smile on his face when Jim sent the message. Mescal gave a little cry and darted into the woods for refuge. The older Sutherlands turned to each other, seeking comfort. Abigail buried her head on the massive heaving chest and sobbed until Matthew's gruff voice ordered, "Get hot water and medicine, Mother. Apache's hand needs bandaging."

"How did this happen?" Jon wanted to know as his mother dried her tears and expertly tended the wound.

A grim smile heightened rather than lessened the tragedy written in Apache's face. "I slipped away, after finding Jim. No one saw me, but Shalimar snorted when I mounted. Three men ran toward us. One called, 'Hey, that ain't Sutherland's horse,' and reached for his gun. I spurred Shalimar, and we rode straight for them. Two leaped out of the way, the third sprawled on the ground, when Shalimar's shoulder hit him. One shot and it creased me."

"Creased!" Jon looked at the deep groove. "Do you think they recognized Shalimar?"

"No. Radford wasn't one of them. These were others I hadn't seen before. No reason for them to connect me with Jim." Apache took up his story. "I knew some of them followed me from the pounding of hooves and the crash of brush. I lost a lot of blood before I was far enough ahead of them and could cover my trail to stop. I crawled in a rock and slept a few hours, then came on home."

Even through his worry and disillusionment about Jim, Jon couldn't but catch the way Apache referred to the Triple S as "home." At that, it was probably the only real home he'd known for years. Jon watched Apache walk across the clearing to his own cabin, wondering why it was two men reacted so differently to adverse circumstances. Out of gratitude, Apache chose to become the Sutherland's defender. Jim, who had been raised in a God-fearing home, who knew right from wrong and bad from good — Jon couldn't finish the thought.

If waiting had been hard before, now it was unbearable — not that Jon thought Jim would repent and return. He just waited with heart in mouth every time a neighbor reported a missing cow or a stolen horse. Several times news of petty raids on lone travelers and even one bank robbery reached the Triple S. Once a man was killed in a holdup. Jon didn't breathe easy until he rode to Daybreak and discovered the man was a total stranger who might or might not belong to the Comstock Gang, as he called them in his mind.

Fickle March grew into April. The earth warmed. Birds came back from their winter abodes and filled the quiet air with song. Squirrels scolded, and signs of new life appeared regularly. Yet spring did not come to the Sutherlands' hearts. Always winter's shadow lay long and thick, like the snow blankets that bowed great tree limbs until they touched the ground and sometimes broke from too great a weight. Laughter came on infrequent visits, and personal solitude reigned.

One bittersweet moment came when the ranch hands whooped into the corral one morning yelling, "Cattle are back!"

In spite of knowing what it meant, Jon couldn't help the thrill shooting through him. He cornered one of the men. "What do you mean, *back?*"

"Just what I say." Dusty, exuberant, the bowlegged man's grin split his grimy face with a white flash. "Funniest thing, Slim 'n' Dave 'n' Shorty 'n' me had ridden to the south pasture area." His hands stilled on the saddle he'd ungirthed and started to throw off. He scratched his head with a tobacco-stained forefinger. "Three riders came yellin' behind enough cattle to start a small ranch. We figured they were headin' for the waterhole and didn't pay no partic'lar attention. All of a sudden the cattle were on our range, and the riders headin' back the way they come."

"What did you do?" Excitement ran through Jon like forked lightning.

"Hollered at 'em and asked where they found the stock." The cowhand's face wrinkled into a prune. "They waved and rode out of sight. First off, I thought it was your brother, 'cause one horse looked like Dark Star, but they were too far away to be sure. 'Sides, if it was, he'd a' answered. Then we thought it musta been some of our boys, but none of 'em were down there. Guess some neighbors found where the herd drifted durin' the winter. One thing sure, 'twarn't rustlers."

Jon started at the conviction in his voice. "How come you're so positive?"

The hand stared at him then roared. "Ho, how many times do cow thieves bring back what they took? An' without ever changin' their brands?" He turned away before Jon could answer. Just as well. His logic would convince the rest of the country there was nothing unusual except the three riders being too busy to stop and pass the time of day.

Jon rode out with Mescal later that day, into a green-and-gold afternoon. Sluggish blood and a stupor of thought that had held Jon prisoner for the weeks since Jim left lifted. "How can a man help having hope on a day like this?" he asked her, guiding King over to one side of the broad trail so Patches could trot alongside. Apache had ridden out again on Shalimar, scouting the area to see if there was any more news of Jim.

Mescal smiled. Jon realized how rare her smiles had become and how he had missed them. How much she'd changed from the active, touchy kid and even the ecstatic engaged girl. A new womanliness rested on her like blooms on a lilac, adding to her natural charm. "If Jim cared enough to send those cattle back, maybe —" Her appealing eyes lifted. "Once you said you'd bring him back, sometime. Would he come home if you went after him?"

She only echoed the same idea that had been playing tag in his brain from the time the cattle reappeared. "I don't know," he told her honestly.

She didn't answer until after they'd come out on a slight rise, and ahead lay the missing herd. "Oh, Jon, look at them! They're beautiful." Awe stood in her voice; her whole body came alive, more alive than Jon had seen her for a long time. "Our cattle and look over there —" She pointed across the tree-dotted meadow. "There are the horses that vanished last fall!"

Jon strained his eyes. Mescal could see things outdoors with an uncanny, farseeing sight. She said Apache had trained her to see, not just to look, as the white people so often did. "Let's ride down there and get them home." He circled to the left, with her close behind. Still it took a good half hour to get to the horses. Not a one that had been gone so long was now missing. Jim had evidently done his work well.

"But at what cost!" Mescal finished his unspoken thought aloud. Jon saw the glitter in her eyes and her white convulsed face as she wheeled Patches and rode the other way to head off one of the horses that didn't appreciate being driven.

"What's this?" Jon's sharp eyes fixed on a tiny white something tangled in the mane of a big bay. "Whoa there, boy." He soothed the skittish stallion with his voice until he could reach the snowflake-sized white patch. "Paper! No bigger than. . . ." He could feel the blood drain from his head, leaving him curiously light-headed.

"A message?" Mescal's breathless voice called. She dug her spurless boot heels into Patches' sides and galloped to Jon. "Is it from Jim?"

He couldn't speak, held it out, watched her congeal at the three words: A WEDDING PRESENT.

"The fiend!" Where Jon had reacted in shocked disbelief, she stormed, "Isn't it bad enough he goes to the devil, breaks your folks' and your hearts? Must he taunt me with it?" Magnificent in her blazing response, Mescal leaned low over Patches' neck. "Get going!" The pinto, galvanized into speed, raced back the way they'd come, leaving Jon to start driving in the returned horses.

Halfway home, he met her coming to him. Red spots still rode her cheeks. Her eyes still shot lightning bolts. But her voice was normal pitch. "Sorry I ran out on you. No need disturbing the folks with this, is there?"

"Not the message. Just the return of the horses and herd." Jon crushed the infinitesimal paper to oblivion and tossed it to the range. "He's doing everything he can to make sure we stay in business — and keep away from him." Corroding bitterness ate into Jon's soul.

"I release you from your promise." The red bloom withered and died from her cheeks.

Ten minutes before, Jon would have sworn he was beyond shocking, no matter what happened. He had been wrong. It was the last thing on earth he expected from Mescal. "You mean . . . ?"

Her chin lifted, her throat was steady. "I mean you are no longer bound by the promise you made to sometime bring him back." She turned Patches without another word, letting him pick his way home.

A hundred yards behind, Jon followed, stunned by Mescal's final acceptance of what he himself would never accept: that Jim wasn't worth it. Winds of protest blew through his body, chilling the marrow of his bones. If even Mescal gave up on Jim, could keep faith that one day his brother would be free of the life binding him? Depressed, sick, Jon cared for the horses but didn't feel he could face Mescal yet, not as she now was. He walked aimlessly into the woods in back of the ranch house and was stopped by some sound that did not belong to the place. He quietly parted the slender branches of aspens, hiding their contents.

Mescal lay half hidden in a circle of compassionate, shivering leaves, crying her heart out.

For a moment only, Jon watched her, transfixed by her grief so strangely in contrast with her last words to him. Then step by noiseless step, he retreated and went back to the corral. By the time she appeared, he had erased every telltale sign of his private turmoil and was able to greet her naturally. There was no trace of tearstains on the smooth cheeks, but her eyes had been freshly washed. Her determined manner didn't fool Jon a bit. She could battle valiantly and without quarter, but she could not change her feelings for Jim.

"Mescal." He stopped what he was doing. "I want you to listen and not interrupt. Then I'll never bring it up again. I promised you I'd bring him back, and I will." He held up a hand to silence her automatic protest. "If you don't want him, then you can decide and tell him so. But because you release me doesn't mean I won't keep my word. I have to. I promised myself as well as you, and someday, when the time seems right, I'm going after him."

With an inarticulate cry she ran past him and into the house.

May brought fresh news of various crimes committed by an unknown person or persons. Jon took the bull by the horns and buttonholed Radford Comstock on the dusty street of Daybreak. "You're sheriff around here, aren't you? When are you planning to do something about what's happening?"

The lean, dark face never betrayed by a flicker anything other than contempt. "From what I hear, the Triple S ain't suffering, so what's your gripe?"

Jon longed to lash out and strike down the reptile before him. "Plenty of others are wondering the same thing. Enough, in fact, that the next time it comes time to get a sheriff appointed, I reckon I'll be applying for that job."

Hate gleamed in the dark eyes watching him. "Thought you aimed to be a preacher."

"Even preachers have been known to kill rattlesnakes — if they curl too close around their boots." Jon stalked off before he could add more, aware of the hostile look boring holes in his back the way

Comstock would probably send bullets flying if he dared.

"He won't forgive me for that," Jon soliloquized on the ride home. "Wonder what he plans to do about it? Sheriff's job doesn't pay much, but Comstock probably thinks it gives him some kind of honor in Daybreak." The threat he'd made popped into his mind. "I might just try for sheriff myself. This'd be a whole lot better place to live."

Comstock's reply to Jon's prodding wasn't long in coming.

Two weeks later Apache rode in on a winded Shalimar. He waited until he got Jon alone and gave him the bad news. "Radford Comstock's got Jim just where he wants him."

Jon mutely stared, heart in his boots.

"He's given out how since the Triple S is the only place not getting raided, stands to mind there's a reason. Since Jim Sutherland 'ain't been heard of' for a time, and rumors have been flying, he's going to get himself a posse and go into the canyon country and 'stop this . . . stealin' for once and all.' "

"So that's his game." Jon dropped heavily to a chair. "I never gave him enough credit for having that much brains. He must have planned it all along." Revenge surged up in a swelling tide. "When do we ride?"

"Tonight. The posse's already getting ready, but it's better for us to go after dark. We'll be between two enemies, remember. The Comstocks aren't going to be any gladder to see us than the posse."

"They'll be even less happy when it's all over," Jon promised through gritted teeth. "Let's see, how many in the Comstock outfit?"

Apache inclined his head. "About a dozen, unless some are on a raid. I wouldn't put it past Radford to set something up to catch Jim red-handed."

Jon fought nausea and checked his rifle. It was against everything in him to go after men with a gun. All his principles said, "Don't kill." Yet what choice had Jim left him? "And in the posse?" he asked.

"Six or eight."

Jon could feel Apache's appraising surveying of him when he laughed harshly. "That makes eighteen or twenty. Odds are about right, I'd say."

"How many of the hands are you asking to ride?"

"None."

Apache grunted, but Jon saw the slight smile that showed he was pleased. "Be ready at nine o'clock."

Eerie clouds covered the moon when Apache, on the big bay, Jon, on a dead black, quietly left the ranch. Shalimar had been ridden too hard to take, and when Jon started to saddle King, Apache stopped him. "Dark horses this night."

Dark horses and dark deeds. Jon had never been torn apart the way he now was. Emotions birthed and died: anger with Jim for getting him into this position; hatred of the Comstocks and the evil they stood for; pity for the folks and Mescal, if his plan didn't work. It was likely neither twin would survive the coming hours, if either the Comstocks or the posse, all cut from the same rotten bolt of cloth, had their way.

Hours in the saddle left him tired and sore. He'd finally given up trying to pray or even considering what lay ahead. What would happen must be allowed to run its course.

An uneasy dawn broke, with rain pouring and a shroudlike gray fog descending, until at times he could no longer see Apache on the unused trail ahead. Once he asked, "Wouldn't it be better for us to get there ahead of the posse?"

Apache only shook his head, ghostly in the misty morning. "No. Let all be together. Surprise is our only real weapon. The posse will have scattered the Comstocks — trust Radford for that. He'll be sure enough noise is made by his hand-picked riders, so his relatives can get away. They've probably been alerted anyway."

The callousness of the sheriff's plan dried Jon's mouth and shut off his inner, insistent voice. What he had to do was wrong. Jim had been right: The only way to kill a snake was to step on it and crush it forever. Jon's throat filled with ashes of fiery dreams to make men listen to a better way of life; when he mounted the black, to save his brother, he destroyed any chance of that.

A lifetime later Apache took yet another of the tortuous turns into what he said was the hideout. How he knew the way, only God knew — and the eagles. "We'll hide the horses here," Apache whispered. "I can see campfires ahead. They have one outside the cabin, a big one." He slid forward on wet leaves that camouflaged and deadened his slow movements, Jon at his heels. "Now we wait."

Jon buried his face in his arms, to still the heavy breathing from crawling and from fear of what lay ahead. When he raised his head, only Apache's warning hand over his lips kept him from crying out. A pine tree stood out clearly in the firelight ahead. Over it hung a limp rope, sinister, suggestive.

Jon clenched his teeth to keep from retching. Across the firelit clearing, Jim stood with both hands over his head. A bearded stranger held a gun on him. Jim's defiant voice cut clearly into the falling night. "I tell you, I wasn't in on any bank robbery yesterday. Cookie can vouch for me." His disheveled hair looked gold in the flickering light.

"That's right." A pallid man spoke up. "Sutherland an' me played cards all afternoon."

"Shut up," his captor snarled. "Inside the cabin, Sutherland. I got a hunch the sheriff'll be along soon." His furtive glance toward the darkened rim where the firelight ended gave away knowledge of a well-laid plot, and Jon shuddered in the darkness.

Jim stepped inside the cabin. Jon could hear the creak of leather and the jingle of spurs. Once Jim mumbled something, but the sound of a sharp blow cut off words. Jon's hair rose, along with his temper. "I'm going in after him," he whispered.

"Wait!" Apache's steel fingers bit into his

arm. A second later the gun-carrying stranger came back outside. He looked both ways then motioned to the cook and another man to go. Cookie glanced toward the cabin.

"Get out of here, you —" The man and two others who stepped from the shadows herded the two off into the woods. Galloping hooves portrayed their rapid departure.

Jon could see it all clearly. Beard would come back, wait for the posse and "try" Jim. "I can sneak in, get him out, and we'll get away before they come," Jon urgently told Apache. "You stay here and give me all the time you can. If you have to, run off any spare horses or ride away yourself and lead them into thinking Jim got away." Before Apache could argue, Jon slipped to his feet, skirted the fire and slid behind the rude cabin, praying there was a window at the back.

His prayer was answered — a window with a heavy shutter had been carved into the logs of the cabin. Jon slid the blade of his hunting knife up, slit the buckskin thongs that held the shutters in place, and laid them on the ground without a sound. He thrust his head and shoulders inside, ignored Jim's low cry, and stepped through onto the dirt floor.

PART III
Sons of Thunder

9

Jim Sutherland pulled back on King's reins. "Whoa, boy." King slowed and stopped at the edge of the home clearing. Jim opened his mouth to call a greeting to Jon and Mescal ahead. It died on his lips when he heard her troubled whisper carried straight to him by the breeze lifting her hair and playing with her eyelashes.

"I really love him, but sometimes I wish — Jon, if only he were more like you!"

Jim barely heard Jon's stunned reply. The clouds he'd ridden for the weeks since he learned Mescal loved him turned to solid earth. In a moment they'd see him. They must never know he'd overheard.

"Don't worry about Jim." He tried to sound amused. He went on to flippantly tell them Radford Comstock would attend the wedding, kissed Mescal's protest away, and walked after her when she ran, forcing a whistle. He knew Jon watched with tortured eyes, told himself fiercely he didn't care. Mescal had chosen, and she was his, not his brother's. Yet her wistful eyes haunted him, and her wish sank deep in his soul. *More like Jon.* His carved lips whitened. Hadn't it been that way ever since he came back? Better if he'd stayed away. He wasn't Jon and never would be. Spineless, refusing to fight — hot tears crowded his eyelids, and he forced them back. No, Jon was none of those things. It took more courage to do what he believed right than to give in.

So what should he do? Day and night the question mocked him. He'd been so sure Mescal and the challenge of making the Triple S a tremendous ranch would be enough to hold him. Why not do nothing? Jon would be gone soon. He and Mescal could go ahead with their plans. Besides, Mescal didn't love Jon, not in the way needed for marriage.

She might, if you were gone.

Cursing, he plunged into frenzied activity. Anything to drown the nagging reminder. Although he tried to hide his knowledge of the conversation, small taunts escaped him, and the last day of February something dark and undeniable rose in him. "I'm riding to Daybreak for a last fling," he announced. Over Mescal's threats and protests, he slipped to the stable, started to throw a saddle on King, and stopped. No. Dark Star would be better for whatever lay ahead. Everyone in the country knew King, while Dark Star could be mistaken for a dozen other local horses.

The ride to Daybreak cleared his mind. He wouldn't go back. Jon once said doing things for someone else was pretty great; well, he'd make himself scarce. He shut his mind and heart to the dull ache when he thought of Mescal. So what if she cared now? In the long run she'd be better off. Even if Jon went ahead and became a preacher, Mescal would have the best man.

"The best man!" His grating laugh shattered his last dream, along with the silence of the woodsy trail. "I'll go whole hog. Send word the best man wins. That'll turn Mescal away from me, and she'll forget in time." He clamped down hard with his teeth, and blood spurted from a cut lip. The pain released some of the pain inside. He mopped at it with his kerchief and rode on.

By the time he reached town, his mood bordered on the dangerous. First thing he did was ride straight to the jail. "Out." He jerked his thumb over his shoulder at the hangers-on surrounding the sheriff. When they'd gone, surprise showing on their ugly faces, he came straight to the point. "Know anyone around here who needs a good man?"

Radford Comstock's sensual, cruel

mouth dropped open. He leaned his dark-clad body back in his chair until his shoulders touched the dirty wall. His wolfish eyes never left Jim's face. "Depends on who that man is — and what he can do."

Jim's reply was to snatch his gun from its holster, flip it toward the sneering sheriff, and put three bullets over his right shoulder, into the wall behind him. A sneaking admiration filled him. Comstock didn't move an inch.

The next moment the room was full of men. "What's going on in here?"

Comstock reached for cigarette makings and drawled, "Sutherland here just killed a spider."

"Three shots in the same hole?" A hawk-eyed man ran his finger in the hole, checked the wall for other holes, and shook his head when he found none. "Musta been *some* spider."

"If you men will get out of here, we'll finish our talk."

Grumbling, the others went back outside. Comstock slowly rolled a cigarette. Jim's sharp eyes noted a slight unsteadiness of the long fingers. The sheriff wasn't as nerveless as he'd thought earlier.

"As we were saying —" Jim paused suggestively.

"So what's wrong with the Triple S that — a man looks for another job?"

A wild idea crossed Jim's mind like a racing mustang. He rejected it, reconsidered. Could he pull it off? His eyes gleamed, and he leaned forward, voice low. "Radford," it was the first time in years he'd called the man anything but *Comstock.* "The Triple S isn't big enough for my brother and me. Besides, some thieving varmints are running off the stock. Not much future there."

A curl of smoke hid Comstock's face, but the razor-keen voice cut through. "Just maybe both those problems could be solved at once."

He'd swallowed the bait whole. Jim exulted, but carefully hid his excitement. "Which means?"

Comstock's casual tone roused the primitive in Jim. "If a good man chose to work for the right people —" He paused and blew another screen of smoke. "I could just about guarantee no more cattle and horses would disappear from the Triple S."

Jim had never wanted anything in his life so much as to launch himself headlong into the bogus sheriff. He forced a light laugh that set his nerves on edge. "Could you also guarantee the return of stock and horses already gone?"

A long silence ensued. Jim held his breath. Had he gone too far? He could feel sweat trickle down his neck. If he gave up Mescal, but could see the Triple S on its feet again, maybe it would be worth turning outlaw. Nothing else he could ever do would show his twin how much he cared. Jon's eyes rose to accuse him and were forced down. There were many ways to fight the Comstocks. Jon could choose his, Jim would do his own deciding. He knew his reasoning was faulty but refused to admit it. If it came to an all-out fight with the Comstocks, he'd probably be killed anyway. Might just as well get something for the folks out of it. At least when he was dead it would be one decent thing he'd done, even though the way it had to be accomplished might not be square.

Comstock's low voice jerked him back to attention. "I'd say as long as a Sutherland stuck with his new boss, even that might be done. I've heard tell Sutherlands are trackers and know every inch of this country, almost as well as Comstocks."

Jim was tempted to tell the gloating man where to get off, but caught himself up sharply. He laughed instead, then shot across the room at a rustle in the leaves outside the jail window. "What was that?"

Comstock reached the window at the same time. "Don't see anything."

"Something made that noise, and there's no wind." Jim pressed his face to the heavy iron bars. His keen eyes examined the clump of pines, whose swaying branches proclaimed any disturbance to high heaven.

The branches moved again, and Jim drew his gun. Then a squirrel leaped from one branch to another and disappeared into the distance.

"Stupid squirrel." Jim sheathed his gun, and swung back to face Comstock. "Well?" The word cracked like a revolver shot.

"Soon as the range is so cattle and horses can be moved, the Triple S stock will be sure to wander back from where they wandered off."

Jim hated the triumph in the smoky black eyes, but hid it. "I'll be around town, whenever my new boss — whoever that might be — wants me." He eased across the filthy floor and into the street, torn between wanting to go back and force a confession of rustling from the sheriff and determination to follow the course he'd laid out for himself. The second impulse won. He headed toward the saloon and met Apache halfway down the street. For a quick moment he wondered if the Indian could have been outside the jail window during the conversation. He shook his head impatiently. Impossible. He'd seen the squirrel; besides, in the time it took him to get down the street, Apache wouldn't have been able to get ahead of him. He dismissed the idea and demanded, "Are you following me?"

"Do you need following?" Was it contempt in the bottomless depths of Apache's eyes?

Jim dropped it. "Are you headed back for the Triple S?"

"Yes. Soon." If there was significance to that, Jim failed to catch it.

"Good. Take this to Jon —" He scribbled, THE BEST MAN WINS — AGAIN, on a torn piece of paper he found in the street. "And tell Mescal Jim says to forget him. Jon will make her a better husband." Something in the steady scrutiny made him add, "I'll be riding out. You can tell Mescal it won't be hard for her to love one twin as well as another." He spun around on his boot heel and left Apache in the street.

Weeks later he reined in Dark Star miles away in the canyons. God must have made the place then forgotten it, he thought.

Piles of rock crouched like mountain lions on both sides of a perilous trail. Overhangs encroached on the trail, at places, until horses could barely get through. The perfect hideout. And the valley beyond defied description: Long, narrow, yet big enough to hide the stock driven in from the other way, over a bare rock trail that held no tracks, lush and green fields broken with trees contrasted strangely with the outlaw band who inhabited it. What a place to live! Jim rode to the rude cabin ahead. If only he could show Mescal this place.

Reality fell on him, a mountain of depression. Mescal would never see this place. No one else he loved would either. The Comstocks guarded it and jealously protected it, even from other outlaw bands. There probably wasn't one man in Arizona outside those brought in by the gang who knew it.

"Except Apache," Jim mused. "Bet he could find it, if he wanted to." A hard-bitten smile split his grim face. "Wouldn't be surprised to have him ride in sometime. Mescal and Jon won't let me get away so easily. Wonder if they're married by now?" He knew he lied when he said it. Yet in no other way could he keep on with the trail he'd chosen to ride. Only knowledge he was doing it for his family kept him from sloping off in the night, now he knew the ways in and out of the valley. He was tired and sick of the small stuff they'd done — a few cattle here, a good horse there. Once Radford gave the order, and the Triple-S stock was sent home, maybe he'd head for New Mexico or Texas, start over. It wasn't as easy squandering his life as he'd thought it would be, and memories of home lay raw and exposed, unless he guarded against them every minute.

A night or two later, a stealthy step behind him caused Jim to turn toward it, gun in hand. Before he could speak, a sinewy hand covered his mouth, and a voice hissed in his ear, "It's Apache."

Jim relaxed, tore himself free. Gladness filled him, quickly replaced with alarm. "You shouldn't be here!"

"Should you, James Sutherland?"

Jim recoiled from the question and whispered, "What do you want?"

"To give you a message." Apache repeated what he'd been told. "Mescal cares nothing for Jon except as a brother. She loves you. She wants a home and freedom from fear."

"I can never give her that." Jim felt ragged breaths bolt through his lungs.

"Tell them — once I take a trail, I don't turn back." He wrenched free of Apache's hand that still lay on his shoulder. "Now get out before you're discovered."

Not even a rustle told of Apache's passing. Jim stood with head bent, ears strained. An oath, then, "Who's that? It ain't Sutherland's horse!" burst into his brain. He leaped forward, ready to defend Apache, if needed. Three of the men Comstock had recently imported raced off in the direction Apache had taken. The next instant Shalimar lunged into view, knocked one man aside, and scattered the other two. One shot ended in a sickening thud. Jim's heart dropped. Was Apache hit?

"After him." Jim leaped astride Dark Star's bare back, senses alert. The others followed, grunting and cursing. He had to be first down the trail, to buy Apache time. He deliberately slowed Dark Star, who must have recognized Shalimar and wanted to run. "This way, you rustlers!" He veered to the left, away from Shalimar's path. The rain had started. By the time morning came, all sign of Apache's trail would be obliterated.

A long time later he gave up in disgust. "No use going on in this downpour!" he told the disgruntled outlaws behind him. "Anyone recognize the horse?"

"Not me."

"Or me."

"Me, neither. We ain't been here long enough," the third new man apologized. "Haw, haw, give us a few weeks an' we'll make a handshakin' acquaintance with every good saddle horse in this country."

They reached the cabin, and the strangers gathered inside, along with some of the regular men, who'd been playing cards, but Jim checked both ways then nonchalantly slipped to the location where that single shot had been fired. A careful search revealed a bullet imbedded in a tree trunk. A slight reddish stain showed where it had gone in. "Must have nicked Apache, but couldn't have done much harm," Jim decided.

The best day of the wilderness sojourn came when Jim and two others drove the Triple S stock home. "Don't anybody get near enough to be recognized," he ordered sharply.

"Don't see how come we steal then take it back," one griped, but Jim's quick gesture toward his gunbelt silenced him. Not a man in camp but what recognized his superior draw and edgy temper. He'd backed off the biggest bully in the outfit, bearded Nil Hathaway, when he caught Nil cheating at cards, and since then the men steered clear of riling him.

It was a poignant moment for Jim when they left the Triple S to head back into the canyons. Radford Comstock had made good his word, loudly boasting he expected to get a hundred times the price of the stock out of Jim's daring and knowledge of the area. His wicked glee even rubbed off on his men, and raid after raid was planned. Now all Jim wanted to do was join the Triple-S hands. When one of them raised one arm, to wave, Jim's heart lurched. Had he been recognized, or had Dark Star given him away? He deliberately waved back, then with a "Hi-yu!" such as a helpful neighbor would give, rode slowly on.

Never thought I'd miss the place so much, Jim confessed to himself. *April's got to be the best month of all — new leaves on the aspens, flowers thinking about growing, and birds and animals coming back alive.* The familiar ache inside expanded. He might ride away from the ranch, but he couldn't ride away from himself. He'd tried it Indian fighting. It hadn't worked now anymore than then.

"Reckon as soon as I can get away, I'll

head off into the lonelies." He gazed south. "Maybe try California then work back to the Tonto." But all his plans were forgotten when he reached camp. "Anything to eat, Cookie?"

"Not much." The disgruntled cook spread wide his hands. "Comstock says he's too busy chasin' outlaws to haul in supplies." He reluctantly checked the chuckwagon and produced a chunk of meat and some cold biscuits. "That'll have to do 'til supper."

"Want me to get you some meat?" Jim patted his rifle.

"You bet." Reluctance died. Jim knew he'd made his first friend among the rustlers. From then on he supplied Cookie with deer, rabbits, and birds. He'd always liked hunting, and it kept him away from camp. Now he'd made up his mind to go, the best way was to allay any suspicions anyone might have, before slipping off.

May scampered by on sunny feet. Jim was almost ready to leave. He'd made an effort to be agreeable lately, and all except Nil Hathaway seemed to relax around him. The bearded giant had never forgiven Jim for showing him up in front of the men, Jim knew. He was careful never to turn his back on the man.

Comstock jerked most of the men from

camp for a gigantic raid one night. He'd ordered Jim to stay behind. "You could be too easily recognized," he stated flatly. "This one's near Daybreak — horses." His flushed face showed he'd been drinking hard.

Uneasiness slid through Jim's veins at the strange look on Comstock's face — half triumph, half anger. Jim decided right there he'd ride out when the others had gone. That afternoon he carefully rolled his few belongings together and hid them near the sheltered nook where he kept Dark Star. He'd moved his horse from the corral after seeing the greedy eyes of some of the men following him, especially Nil's. He spent the afternoon playing cards with Cookie, tossed and turned during a miserable night too black to hazard the trail out, and headed away from camp the next day, in a gray fog. He hadn't gone far when he ran smack into Nil and part of the gang riding in.

"Where you think you're goin'?" Nil challenged, jaw stuck out.

"After meat."

"When all the game's lyin' down under trees?" Nil's scarred face contorted into a knowing smile.

"You calling me a liar?"

The men on both sides of Nil broke

away from him at the menace in Jim's voice and the steadiness of his left hand, holding Dark Star's reins. Jim could see the temptation to draw in the pale blue eyes and the final decision not to push it. "Naw. Just be sure you come back." He laughed coarsely and moved on.

Jim didn't dare try for a break after that. Tension mounted. There had been something strangely triumphant in Nil's face, the same look Radford Comstock had worn when he gave the orders for the last raid. Jim shrugged. Nothing to do but wait. He succeeded in scaring up a deer, killed it, and packed a haunch back to camp. He caught the disbelieving stare Nil bestowed on him and cheerfully told Cookie, "I'll get the rest for you later, unless one of these wild raiders want to pack it in." He rubbed his hands over the fire. "Feels good."

The rain stopped, but the fog remained. Jim brought in the rest of the meat, then ate a silent supper. When darkness fell, he stood and yawned, "Me for the sack." He turned from the giant fire Cookie used outside when he could.

"Hold it, Sutherland." Nil whipped out his Colt. "I been deputized to arrest you for killin' a man in yesterday's bank robbery." He flung back his steaming coat. A silver star bounced firelight beams into Jim's face.

Jim laughed scornfully. "You know better than anyone I wasn't in any bank robbery. Cookie can vouch for me." He ran one hand through his hair, tensed to spring, if there was any opening.

"That's right. Sutherland an' me played cards all afternoon."

"Shut up!" Nil glared at Cookie. "Inside the cabin, Sutherland. I got a hunch the sheriff'll be along soon."

So that was it. Jim hesitated on the doorsill, ready to turn. A harsh jab reminded him of the futility of it. He went on, suffering himself to be securely tied and thrown on a bunk in the corner. Through the open doorway, he could see a long, limp rope dangling from the big pine. He went cold to his toes. Comstock would come, probably with a posse. They'd have trumped-up charges, and hang him. No matter what Cookie said —

"Get out of here, you!" With a mighty effort, Jim raised up in spite of his bound hands and feet. Cookie and Tom were being pushed off to the woods. The sounds of pounding hooves indicated their escape.

A bitter smile crossed Jim's face. Twice

before he'd been on the verge of death. Both times Apache had come. This time would do it. There was no Apache to rescue him. The enormity of what he'd done swept over him. Would any of them ever recover from the shock of learning he had been hung? The damning evidence against him would linger in their memories forever. The one time he'd been innocent, and he was going to hang, be dragged back dead as an example by a sheriff who would loudly proclaim his victory over rustling and robbing!

"God, what have I done?" Jim licked parched lips. "And what will happen to my family and Mescal?" Too-vivid scenes painted themselves on the dimly lit cabin walls: Mother, dying from the shock; Dad, hair turning whiter, shoulders stooped with shame; the Triple S robbed and ruined; Mescal — he shut his eyes but couldn't keep out the images of the future. What a devilish way to get Mescal. Radford Comstock had planned it all along. With him out of the way and Jon disposed of. . . .

A slicing sound interrupted Jim's hell on earth. He peered across the cabin. A shutter disappeared. Another. A man's head and shoulders came through the window.

"Jon!" It rattled in Jim's throat.

The next instant his twin was beside him, cutting his bonds, freeing him, then gathering Jim into an embrace that threatened to choke the breath from him.

"Don't try to talk," Jon whispered. "Comstock and a posse are on their way. Apache's outside, with the trail in blocked. He'll ride off and make them think it's you, if he has to. Come on!"

"Too late!" Jim heard shots and the voices of men. "Go, Jon, save yourself. I'll hold them off." He met his brother's blazing eyes. "I'm guilty of small raids, nothing more. I've not killed, and I wasn't in on the bank robbery yesterday. Radford wouldn't let me go."

"Is that square?" An unearthly light whitened Jon's face.

"God as my witness!" Jim's talonlike fingers gripped Jon's shoulders. "Now that the cattle are back, I was going to ride out. California or somewhere. I'm not good enough for Mescal, never was. Tell her I really loved her — and hope someday you and she . . . ," his voice failed.

"Mescal never loved anyone but you, Jim." Jon half dragged him across the floor. A volley of shots and the steady drumbeat of a running horse stopped him cold.

"That's Apache and the bay. Come on!" He almost jerked Jim from his feet.

"How could Sutherland get untied?" a new voice roared. Jim recognized Radford Comstock's cry and dug in his heels. "Too late, I tell you. Save yourself." He snatched the revolver from Jon's holster and sprang back to the bunk. "If you're caught, it will mean both of us. Mother couldn't stand that. For God's sake, go!"

"For *God's* sake?"

Jim caught the tone in Jon's voice. Smothering fear, such as not even death could bring, pinioned him to the bunk. From faraway he heard Jon's whisper, "Good-bye, pard."

Something exploded in his head, white-hot, crippling. Through the waves he heard a voice, "Check that cabin and stop who-ever's on that horse!"

On the brink of consciousness, Jim felt someone fumbling with his clothes. He couldn't move. He must save Jon. He started to cry out and was vaguely aware of cloth being stuffed in his mouth. He felt misty air, a mighty shove. Jim Sutherland, hung for rustling.

Another explosion inside him. Was it his heart tearing apart from regret?

Then — eternal blackness.

10

Thousands of hammers beat in Jim's brain. He moaned and tried to open his eyes. When he succeeded, he thought he'd gone blind. Or was he dead? He remembered that suspension in space. The muffled sound he knew came from his own throat made it hard to breathe. He reached with trembling fingers and tore the gag from his mouth. Forcing himself to close his eyes, then reopen them, he saw nothing but blackness. The only sound was the steady drip, drip, drip of the mist turned to rain.

Where was he?

He tried to sit up, failed, and tried again. His head brushed wet leaves. He rubbed his eyelids clear of rain and finally got to his feet. What was he doing lying in a cluster of wet aspens?

Little by little it came back: the accusation, Jon's arrival — "Jon!" He shook his head violently and cleared the mental fog but not the dull ache. His exploring hand came away wet from the back of his head. What had happened after the explosions in his head? The stains were not water, but sticky ooze he knew had to be blood.

With returning consciousness came caution. Why was camp deathly quiet? He dropped to all fours and inched out of the thicket. His searching fingers touched the rough logs of the cabin. He must be behind it. Jim slid forward, taking care not to rustle. It might be a trap.

He was around the cabin now. The dim glow of a dying cooking fire barely lifted the shadows. It was enough to show his reaching arm. He recoiled violently. Where was his coat? This was Jon's. A premonition of something terrible awaiting him drove him on, more cautious than ever. For minutes he lay still, watching the firelit area. At last he was satisfied it was empty. The gang had gone. Then why did this chill grip him in claws of suspense? Why was he wearing Jon's coat?

Again he slipped forward, eyes straining for he didn't know what. Across the circle of pale light something moved. Jim grabbed for his gun, clawed at emptiness. The revolver he'd taken from Jon was gone.

An ominous sawing sound halted him. He barely breathed. Then when his nerves screamed for release from whatever evil spell lay ahead, the almost-dead fire eagerly pounced on one untouched log. A great flare of flame brightened the camp. Jim could feel blood pounding in his brain. The next instant, "Apache!" Jim sagged with relief, but only for a heartbeat.

Apache's tragic face accused him from above a long, inert form.

Jim's blood slowly turned to ice. His breath rattled in his throat. "Not . . . ?"

"Your brother." Never had Apache been more magnificent than when he strode forward, carrying the lifeless body of Jon Sutherland.

"But, I don't understand!" Jim backed away, unable to tear his fascinated gaze from the gruesome burden, protesting with every cell of his sickening body.

"He took your place!" Apache hissed. "Worthless white man, your brother took your shirt, your coat, *and your punishment!*"

"No!" It echoed through the trees, returned to mock him. Jim could feel terror mount. "It isn't true!" He wildly ran forward, ignoring his spinning head and his churning stomach. With a mighty grasp, he tore back the canvas tarp Apache had mercifully drawn over Jon.

His twin's convulsed face, still strangely radiant, stared up at him.

"No!" Jim shrieked. He dropped the tarp and fell to the dirt. His revolting stomach and breaking heart took control. A long time later, spent, sick, crazed with grief, he sat up and wiped his streaming face. Memory of a year-old conversation taunted him. Jon's voice, *"Suppose saving my life meant taking my place and dying yourself so I could go on living?"* His own, *"Not many men would do that."* Jon saying, *"One did."*

Jim writhed in agony. *"One did. One did. One did."* He hadn't cared about that one. Now his own brother had done the same. He understood Jon's repetition of his own plea, "For God's sake," just before —

"He must have knocked me out and pitched me through the window." Was that his voice, that shaking, pitiful whisper?

"Yes." Apache's inflamed eyes never left him. "While I was leading the gang away, so he could save you, your brother was dying for your crimes."

"I was innocent." Even in his own ears it sounded craven.

"Perhaps this time." Apache gently covered Jon. Without another word he picked him up and walked away. At the edge of the firelight, he stopped. Without turning he asked, "Are you man enough to go home with me and tell your parents and Mescal what happened, or must I protect you again, the way Jon —" He let the sentence hang in the damp air.

I can't go home, ever! Jim's soul burst forth. The words died behind his lips. Despising himself, sick, aching in body and mind and heart, he followed Apache.

Only once on the long, mournful ride home did Jim speak. "Will we be trailed?"

"Why should we be? Radford Comstock and his snakes killed Jim Sutherland, didn't they?"

A new spear impaled Jim. He didn't answer, but his numbed mind turned it over and over. He was dead. So far as anyone except Apache knew, Jim Sutherland was dead. Better if he had been. Wasn't there someone in a Bible story Dad used to read, some guy who'd been dead and lived again? What had that man done when he found himself alive when he should have been dead? A vista of endless, torturous years lay ahead. What would he do with the life Jon had restored at such a terrible cost?

He couldn't think, couldn't decide. First he must face the family.

It was worse than he expected: the joy on Mescal and his folks' faces turning to white horror, the blank stares as he tried to stammer, "I didn't know. . . . He knocked me cold. . . . I tried to make him go. . . ." blended into nothingness. When Jim could stand no more, he wheeled Dark Star and bolted. Anything to get away. He'd brought Jon's body home. Now he would leave them before reproach and hatred could replace their love for him and what he had brought about by his rebellion and pride. He spurred Dark Star to a gallop and didn't stop until he could hear the horse breathing hard. Then throwing the reins over Dark Star's head, Jim sprawled on the ground, clutching handfuls of pine needles and earth. A paroxysm of shock, disbelief, and horror held him until at last sheer despair and fatigue claimed him.

He awoke to Apache's veiled glance. "What are you doing here?"

A contemptuous smile crawled over Apache's face. "I am to go with you."

Jim sprang to his feet, fists clenched. "Just whose idea was that?"

"Mescal's."

It took the fight from Jim. *Why?* The world hung on Apache's reply, and Jim felt blood in his mouth from clamping down on his set lips.

"She said I must give you a message and

remind you of it every time you forget." Steel underlined every word. "Mescal said, 'Tell Jim he no longer owns himself. He has deprived the world of someone whose living would have made it a better place. And now. . . .' "

Jim's nerves tightened until he thought he'd break the way a guitar string snaps under tension. "Well?"

Apache's inscrutable eyes fixed themselves on Jim's face. "Now he must take Jon's place."

Jim couldn't grasp what he was hearing. "Take Jon's place! Me?" His harsh laugh ground into the dark gray day.

"I know you cannot do it. Mescal says you must." Apache folded his arms. "White man, I hate what I am to do, but I will do it. She saved my life. I saved yours, then you saved mine. Now your brother chose to give his own life that you might live. I will eat and sleep and stay with you day and night until the debt is paid. Then I will never see you again — and give thanks for it!"

The finality of the sentence Mescal had pronounced made Jim shiver. It was too incredible to believe — that Mescal ordered him to take Jon's place!

"Come." Apache turned. For the first

time Jim saw King and Shalimar were saddled and packed.

"Let Dark Star go. He will return home."

Jim found his voice, tried to put scorn in it, failed miserably. "Where are you taking me on Mescal's orders?"

Apache's somber eyes turned north and east. "Once your body was healed by the desert. Now its voices cry out for revenge. We will go back to the valley behind the waterfall. There you can think." He swung his gaze to Jim. "If as Mescal believes, there is any hope for you to become a man, it will be there." He motioned Jim to Shalimar and easily swung astride King.

Jim started to protest, shrugged. What difference did it make? It would be as easy to dispose of himself one place as another. No one who had done what he did had a right to live. Yet through his pain and loathing floated Mescal's face. He could almost see her white lips as she pronounced judgment — to give him a final chance in a trial by fire. Once he had said he would return to the desolation of the canyon country. He'd laughed and joked about it. Now he began the long journey. Would he ever make the even longer journey back?

He closed his eyes to the past, future,

and present, lapsed into deliberate blankness, and followed Apache.

In many ways the trip was a repeat of the one before. Then he'd been oblivious to his surroundings because of physical weakness and pain. This time he saw little in the tremendous willpower it took to erase memory of Jon's face as he last saw it. It intruded between him and King ahead, always leading deeper into the wounded land. It crept between him and the nightly campfires. It appeared and vanished in the morning mist and the evening twilight. Something in the apparition's eyes always called, demanding that which Jim couldn't give. Apache spoke little. Was it part of his plan to let Jim go insane, bury him far away from the Triple S, and finally bring peace to the Sutherlands?

Jim shook off the recurring apprehension of the thought. Apache would be true. He would repay Mescal with every fiber of his being. He might secretly despise Jim, but it would not stop him in his pursuit of duty.

At first the landmarks they passed meant little, but gradually Jim began to see the places crying out for his attention. He recognized where Apache left him and went for pack burros. He noticed marks along the trail, telling him they were getting near their destination. The homesteader's cabin was empty. Had he been run out by thieves or given in to the relentless weather? It didn't matter. Jim wouldn't have wanted to see him if he'd still been there. Every unusual noise on his overstrained system brought a whiplike response. It wasn't until after they reached the waterfall curtain hiding the valley that would be stage for whatever lay ahead that Jim lost some of the numbness shielding him.

What the blood-red and crimson cliffs hadn't been able to do, that glistening waterfall accomplished. Returning life and feeling made his former anguish nothing. When he rode through the waterfall and into the verdant valley, not all the streams on his face were from the fall.

"Look!" he pointed to the closely grouped cottonwoods. "The deer have come back."

"Life goes on." Apache's ponderous statement did nothing to bring light to his eyes. He hadn't smiled once since Jim had discovered him by the cabin, days before.

For one unreal moment it seemed time had turned back almost a year. The same sage smell tantalized Jim. The same wild flowers waved greetings in the gentle breeze. Even the burros and horses rolling in the grass, when they'd been unpacked, were the same sight they'd been there.

Jim did his share of the work setting up camp, then wandered off. He had to be alone. He could never forget or even think when Apache was near, never accusing in words anymore, but a constant reminder of tragedy. Jim aimlessly followed deer trails, noticing wryly how this time the deer were wary. Last summer they'd been unafraid. They'd learned from experience, from seeing many of their number hunted and killed.

Cold sweat formed, although the day had grown scorching. Jim's teeth chattered. Could he ever kill anything again, even to eat, without remembering? He clamped his mouth tight against the familiar gorge rising within him, determined not to give in as he had before. It was useless. Retching, sobbing, he collapsed on the ground until the spell was over. Perhaps in time it would become less violent. All he could presently do was fight it.

Days dragged leaden feet, each hour torment. Unless Jim spoke directly to Apache, the Indian never talked. It was just as well. Jim had nothing to say, no defense against memory. Nights were worse. The voices he'd heard calling intensified to a roar that drowned out even the waterfall's moan.

Night after night Jim awakened bolt upright, shivering, clutching his blanket, and dripping sweat. Until he could convince himself it had been an owl or night creature, he never slept. He became gaunt, haggard, and great silver patches tinged the hair at his temples. The face peering back from the stream was years older than it should have been.

Only once did he rail against Apache. It came suddenly. The weight of the days and nights, coupled with regret, burst forth in one mighty demand, "Why don't you go back and tell them I am dead?" He felt foam rise to his lips. "It's true enough, I *am* dead — a walking dead man."

Apache didn't deign to reply, but the next morning, when Jim awoke, something hard and square pressed into his outflung hand. A carefully wrapped package tied with string lay on the edge of his tarp.

"What's this?" He spoke to empty air. Apache was nowhere around.

"Stupid to feel afraid of opening it," Jim muttered. Yet he let the package lie until he had breakfast of bacon and biscuits then shaved a week's growth of beard. His heart thumped when he fumbled with the string. The brown paper wrapping fell back. Jim scrambled back as if it had contained a rattler.

Jon's well-worn Bible dropped from his helpless hands and fell open before him.

"No!" His cry was a repetition of the one he had uttered when he had seen his lifeless twin. He let the book lie and rushed headlong into the cottonwoods, stumbling over downed branches, slapping leaves out of his way. Their ooze coated his fingers with their sticky substance, the way the blood from his head wound, where Jon hit him, once coated the same hands. Great, tearing sounds issued from his chest. "Why does everything remind me of it?" Bitter laughter grew into maniacal screams. Had Mescal sent that Bible, or was it Apache's idea of a fitting end to his sanity? Either way it had succeeded. Still shrieking, Jim sank into a stupor that at least quieted his torment.

He never mentioned the Bible to Apache. When he returned to camp, with set face, he gingerly moved it aside with the toe of his boot. He carefully saw to it the tarp covered it from rain but refused to pick it up. Yet the next morning he had rolled over and could feel it under his arm. Teeth imbedded in his lower lip, he reached for it. A flood of feeling engulfed him. It was all he had left of Jon, except Jon's shirt and jacket, carefully stuffed in the bottom of his saddlebags. Slowly he drew it out, noting the way it fell open to marked passages he couldn't read for the red haze in his eyes. He closed the cover and put it under his pillow.

Several days later, Jim waited until Apache left camp. Many times the Indian disappeared for hours, leaving Jim in full possession of the camp. It was pleasant: bordered by cottonwoods, a few larger trees, and the greenness of grass still tasty to the animals who grazed nearby. Summer hadn't yet clutched the earth with heat, and the stream chuckled its way by over red stones. The hum of bees and call of birds added to the charm.

Jim lounged on his bedroll and cautiously took out the Bible. Some of the horror of the past faded, and when Jon's face etched itself on his mind, no rush of nausea accompanied it. The same steady look was in Jon's eyes, but the condemnation Jim had read there before seemed strangely missing. Jon looked more the way he had during those early winter days when they planned their futures around the home fires.

Jim scratched his head. "Wonder if I

could find in here whatever made Jon the way he was?" He awkwardly turned pages, reading here and there some of the places Jon had marked. They seemed scattered and disjointed. Jim sighed and put the Bible away.

Yet day after day, when Apache restlessly roamed the valley, Jim dug out the Bible. He couldn't say he got that much from laboriously picking out the verses. He'd always hated reading, while Jon loved it.

"Why learn all this stuff?" he'd protested angrily against his mother's teachings. "I can ride and shoot and rope. What else do I need?"

His mother remained firm. "No son of mine will be illiterate. You'll learn to read and write and figure enough to make sure you aren't cheated in your cattle deals. Now get to it and no more sass out of you, young man!"

"It's not so bad," Jon interspersed. His blue eyes glowed. "Some of those stories are about battles and stuff."

"Yeah, you read about them, and I'll fight them!" Jim taunted, but Jon only grinned. "I get the best of the bargain."

Jim snapped his book of memory shut. He'd fought all right, and Jon had lost because of it. He sighed and went back to his reading.

Now the night voices changed. Along with wildlife cries came new voices — Mescal's, charging him with the responsibility of not being his own man but bound to replace Jon in some way; Radford Comstock's, gloating. This brought him out of his reverie in a hurry. With Jon, Apache, and himself gone, what was happening at home? How could he have allowed even his own misery to lure him away? But what if he went back? Comstock would bring charges again and. . . .

Jim felt his heartbeat quicken. Apache had told him, "They've killed Jim Sutherland, haven't they, why should we be trailed?" The rankling memory brought daring back to the battle-torn Jim. Suppose he accepted in life the identity Jon had given by his death?

"Impossible!" Jim grunted and lay back down but the haunting idea refused to budge. Like a squirrel in a cage, it circled, reversed, circled again. From early childhood he and Jon had delighted in fooling everyone except their folks and Mescal. If they chose to dress alike and watch the way they talked and walked, not another soul on earth, except Apache, could have told them apart. What was to prevent him from becoming Jon Sutherland and protecting his family?

All night long he accepted and rejected the plan, weighing the pros and cons, unable to sleep. When dawn broke and Apache's moccasined feet noiselessly stole away for his vigil in some unknown part of the lonely canyon, Jim followed him. "Wait."

The tall frame hesitated at the brink of the stream.

"Apache," Jim wondered if his pounding heart was loud enough for Apache to hear. "What if I went back — as Jon?"

Apache spun toward him.

Jim could see that for once the Indian had been shocked from his impassive calm. He rushed on, "Only four people know us apart. Everyone else thinks I'm dead and Jon's alive. I can't live wondering what's going on back at the Triple S. Comstock won't let Mescal alone." His fingers clenched and his lip curled. "Neither will he leave the stock on the range. Without a strong hand to protect it, how can the riders stick and fight off the Comstocks? We need to be there."

Apache's expressive twist of his head followed a grim surveillance of Jim from boot toes to tousled hair. "You think you can be the man your brother was?" He half turned, as if to end the conversation.

"You know how to shove a keen blade in a man," Jim flared.

Satisfaction filled Apache's face. "See? You anger too easily."

Jim's grand plan curled but refused to wither. "I know I can't be Jon, but maybe I can fool others into thinking I am. I'll know myself how poorly I play his part, but does that matter?" He warmed to the idea again. "Look, I'm desperate. I have to do something — not just stay out here and rot inside from the sun and regret." He bent his head. When he raised it again, an odd look rested on Apache's face. Jim tried to interpret it and failed. It couldn't be approval, could it? He shrugged. "Can you burn a tiny scar over my left eye? Jon had one."

"I can. But you forget something." The inexorable Apache gave no quarter.

"What?" Jim rose to the challenge. "With the scar and being on guard all the time, why can't it be done?"

Apache lifted one hand, pointed to the sky. "Your brother planned to preach."

Sickening defeat downed Jim. He'd forgotten how the whole country knew Jon's dream and waited until he was ready to lead them. He turned and bolted from Apache, a wolf fleeing from danger. As he passed his bedroll he snatched Jon's Bible to him and clutched it for a talisman. For hours he walked and ran, pursued by his own soul. Sometimes he tried to read, shook his head, and gave it up. At other times he rested on rock outcroppings, from weariness of body and soul. Even as his original idea had been accepted and rejected a dozen times, a newer, outrageous idea form was squashed and re-formed to entice him.

Could he become the minister Jon had wanted to be?

"Never!" He lifted his face to the sky, almost afraid to look up. Surely a bolt of lightning should strike him for even considering such a thing. "I don't know much about religion, but it would be blasphemy, a man like me daring to. . . ." He couldn't even finish the thought coherently.

It wouldn't be *you,* a small breeze whispered. Jim Sutherland is dead, remember? If you should carry out your plan, it would be the same as if Jon had lived to do it. Remember what Mescal said? *You must take Jon's place.*

"Not literally!" Jim cried. Yet the seed was planted. Despite the burning rays of late afternoon, somehow it sank deeper in his soul and flourished. By the time the distant red rimrock turned purple with evening and a lavender haze filled the valley, it was ready to grow and bloom. Jim started back to camp and met Apache on the way. After long minutes of silent walking, Jim paused near the edge of the stream. "Tomorrow Jon Sutherland goes home." He waited for Apache's protest. It didn't come. "Did you hear me?" Jim demanded, although he knew Apache had.

"I hear, white man." Apache gazed at him through the gloom, "Tomorrow Jon Sutherland returns from the dead."

11

For the fourth time Apache and Jim rode the trail between southeastern Utah and the Triple S. This time Jim's watching eyes missed nothing. Every rabbit or ground squirrel that moved caught his glance. Each tumbling weed and sagebrush clump came in for a share of attention. He couldn't explain, even to himself, yet somehow he was alive. He lifted his face to the southwest. Instantly his elation turned to foreboding. He'd gambled all his life, but never like this. This time he was gambling with his life and for the Triple S.

"I have to win," he whispered passionately to Shalimar. The horse whinnied in response, but Jim had already drifted back into his churning thoughts. First he had to meet his folks and Mescal. Fear that had nothing to do with death gnawed into him. They might turn him out, order him away, as the murderer he was. He set his jaw. He had to meet them truthfully and tell them what he planned to do. First he'd thought he might just go ahead and drop clues along the way through Daybreak but rejected the idea. For once he'd be square and do it right.

His dusty fingers explored the tiny scar Apache had inflicted. He'd known by the Indian's grunt he was pleased, after a few days, when it healed. It had given Jim courage to ask, "Will I pass?"

"Perhaps — on the outside."

Jim hated the note in Apache's voice but knew it was justified. Now it lay in his own hands to change things. It wouldn't be easy. It meant controlling a temper he had never tried to check, acting the way Jon would in like circumstances.

Jim sighed, and Shalimar's ears perked up. It would be so much easier just to blast his way into Daybreak, kill off Radford Comstock and as many of his gang as possible, then ride off, if he were still able. "Can't do it, old boy." He twisted his hand in the tangled mane. "Wonder if I can stand the inaction?"

The same question rode sidesaddle with him through the weary miles and past Daybreak. Try as he would, Jim could not feel prepared for what lay ahead. Uncertainty had always given him the urge to crash ahead against obstacles. This time he didn't even know what they'd be.

Once they left Daybreak, every hoofbeat drummed in Jim's heart. He relived former scenes: Here was where that miserable borrowed horse had bolted. Over there was where he'd first seen Apache — He rudely came to the present when Apache ordered, "Stop!" The Indian and King turned to statues, and Jim followed suit, peering through the trees to see what had alarmed Apache. Apache's face gleamed, and he slid from the saddle, motioning Jim to do the same. Noiselessly they crept forward, Jim's heart doing double time without knowing why — until a low cry from a clearing ahead chilled the marrow of his bones. Mescal! His muscles tensed to spring and protested when Apache's bearlike grip stopped him. Apache moved a little and urged Jim forward, but dropped his arm only to cover Jim's mouth.

Jim choked against the strong hand. Hatred pounded in his temples. In the center of the clearing Radford Comstock stood, braced on both feet, iron grip holding Dark Star's reins. Mescal glared down at him, anger spilling into her flushed face and dark eyes. "Get your hands off him!" She lifted the riding whip she never used and slashed him across the face. Twin welts followed the second blow; then blood spurted.

Comstock fell back but never loosened his hold.

"Let go, I tell you!" Roused to fury, Mescal hit again and again, until Comstock dropped the reins but grabbed the whip, jerked Mescal off balance, and hauled her off the snorting, terrified animal.

Jim leaped to his feet, but Apache seized him in a grip stronger than Comstock's on Mescal. "Wait!" he warned. "You are Jon — remember?"

Though he was almost berserk, it was the one note that could stop Jim. The entire future hung on the next few moments. He must not fail. Before he moved into the clearing, Comstock bellowed, "You devil! All I wanted to do was talk." He shook her fighting body hard.

"Talk!" Mescal blazed back. "The way you've wanted to talk every time you've waylaid me?" Midnight hair set off her white face.

Dark color rolled through the scarred face. "It's your own fault." His hoarse voice echoed through the still air. "I told you I'd marry you proper, but no, you won't have nothin' to do with decent folk, but throw it in my face you loved Jim Sutherland!" A wicked laugh followed. "That rotten thief was hanged for bein' an outlaw."

Jim's involuntary spurt of joy turned to black despair and madness, but Mescal's retort cut through his passion, "Decent folk? Radford Comstock, you're nothing but a cheap rustler who hanged J-Jim Sutherland on a trumped-up charge!" Her break sent chills through the listening man, pride for her defense of him. "Yes, I loved Jim Sutherland, and I always will. Even if I didn't, do you think I'd wipe the muck of the corral off on you?" She jerked hard and freed herself. In one bound she was after Dark Star who'd shied away from the fracas. Comstock leaped after her, then stopped. His eyes bulged. Mescal had snatched a rifle from Dark Star's saddle, aimed it at his middle, and in one motion, cocked it.

"Hold on! I didn't mean —"

"You've gone too far this time," Mescal spit it through clenched teeth. "When I tell how I shot you in self-defense. . . ." Her eyes turned red.

Comstock's livid face and working mouth were almost ludicrous. "You're not goin' to shoot me!" Disbelief settled over his features.

"Why not?" Her question bounced into the air, echoed and disappeared. "I'd kill any skunk in my way, and you've tried to maul me for the last time — ever." Her finger slowly pressed against the trigger, and Comstock stumbled back, tripped, and fell heavily. Groveling in the needle-strewn earth, he cravenly pleaded, "Maybe Sutherland wasn't in on that robbery. Anyone can make a mistake, an' —"

Jim shook off the mingled desire to shout in glee at Mescal's courage and fear she might really kill Comstock. He had too many relatives who'd come after her. It was time for the resurrection. He took a deep breath and strode forward before he could think anymore.

The reaction was instantaneous. Comstock sagged as if he had been shot through. His mouth dropped, his face turned dirty yellow.

Mescal gave a little cry. The rifle barrel wavered, turned a little aside. Her involuntary tightening of fingers fired the gun, but the bullet whistled harmlessly past the crouching Comstock. "J—"

"Yes, it's *Jon,* home at last." His eyes warned her, and he took the rifle from her hands to train it on Comstock. "What's all this about?"

For all Comstock could get out, he'd become permanently dumb. His protruding eyes still held shock. When he finally mustered words, he said, "You, you ain't been seen since —" He couldn't go on.

"Since you murdered my brother for something he didn't do," Jim told him caustically. Inspiration struck. "Unless you swear before these witnesses that my brother was innocent — *and he was.*" Truth rang in Jim's voice, remembering Jon's sacrifice. "I can't speak for what will happen to you." The rifle never wavered as he ejected the spent shell, and a new bullet dropped in place.

Some of Comstock's natural bravado crept back into his mocking laugh. He stood and dusted himself off. "I reckon no preacher's goin' to shoot me, at least not when there're others around to see, even if they are family and a stinkin' Indian."

Jim's whole plot lay imperiled by the insult. Only Apache's quiet, "That won't hold a 'stinkin' Indian' back," saved Jim. He shot a look at Mescal, rigid as a fence-post, then the menacing Apache. "You were saying?"

Apache took one step closer, slid his knife into his palm, and eyed its glitter.

Comstock gave in. He ran his tongue over his lips and muttered, "Like I said, a man can make a mistake." He inched backwards to where a huge bay stood tied to a pine.

"Get out of the country, and take your scum with you," Jim ordered. "Otherwise I'll turn Apache loose on you."

Comstock's dark face shot lightning bolts, but he didn't answer, just swung up on the horse and spurred him. But before he was out of earshot, he called back, "Next time it won't be two to one."

"Three to one," Jim yelled with a roaring laugh. "Seems to me Mescal was doing fine all alone, outlaw!"

The clattering of hooves and a dying curse dwindled into silence. Jim turned to Mescal. "Are you all right?"

Great gulfs of darkness without their golden specks greeted him. "Why did you come back?" Her terrified whisper cut him to the heart. Even after everything, when he had heard her defend him, Jim hadn't been able to control his leap of hope. Now it snuffed out, leaving him a cardboard character with a part to play.

"I'll tell you at home." He paused in the act of helping her mount. Her burst of defiance had gone; he could see in the way her shoulders sagged. "Will I be welcome?"

"Yes."

It kept him together through the ride

home. The scene had left him so numb he could feel nothing. He did notice things were far greener than the previous summer. Evidently there had been rain. A little feeling of relief melted one corner of his frozen state when he saw the tranquility of his home. No signs of strife or war marred its usual peace.

From numbness to burning life, Jim made the jump in one giant leap when his father stepped from the porch. Matthew Sutherland didn't extend his hand, but his voice boomed, "So you've come back." He betrayed neither joy nor surprise, although Jim noted the new lines in the craggy face, the heaviness of his father's carriage.

"If you'll have me, but not Jim." His muddled explanation died in Abigail's arms. "My son, my son!" she cried from the doorway, and he cleared the porch in one bound. Head buried in her apron, the final bitter drop of his deeds reproached him. A long time later he lifted his face to his father. "Dad," a tremor shook him against his best intentions, "I've come home, but with a plan. Let me tell you what it is, and then you can have your say."

To gain time he looked around the small circle. Apache had dropped to the top step, immovable as the big pine in the yard.

Mescal showed signs of the trail encounter, and he couldn't read her expression. Mother still kept her hand on his arm, as if afraid he'd vanish. Dad —

He cleared his throat. "It's my fault Jon's dead, sure as if I'd pulled the trigger." The early agony threatened to overcome him, but he fought until his brow turned clammy and raised his hand against whatever his father had been going to say. "Wait. I can't undo anything. But Mescal sent word I didn't belong to me anymore. She's right. I owe it to Jon to pay my debt any way I can. I about went crazy in the desert, trying to shut out its voices calling for me to do something, anything. I decided I'd come back, as Jon." He ignored the collective gasp from his audience and doggedly went on. "The only thing is, Jon aimed to preach. That means I have to, too, or I'll never get away with it."

"You reckon on saving your skin by playing at preaching?" His father's words slashed as Mescal had slashed Comstock.

"No!" Jim sprang to his feet, horrified. "If it was just me, I'd rather take a beating. It's the only way I can help save the Triple S — and Mescal." He rapidly sketched in the scene in the clearing. "I can't guarantee Comstock will even ride off. He's banking on my being a weakling and you're being so cut up over your son's death you're worthless. It's for you, Dad, and for Mom and Mescal, not for me!" All the weeks of hurt fused into a lump in his throat. If Dad didn't believe him, what was life worth, anyway?

Slowly the hostility for his son left Matthew Sutherland's face. The beginning of a tortured smile fought at the corners of his lips. He asked, "Then it's not being irreverent, what you plan to do?"

"I hope not." Jim forced himself to meet his father's searching stare. "If it is, I'll have to pay the price. I don't know how else I can be worth anything, alive or dead." Bitterness crept in, and he tried to hide it. "It's all I can think of." He saw the disbelieving way his father shook his head then looked at Mother and caught fire.

"Son, Comstock was right. I'd about given up fighting. With you back, and with Apache, maybe the Triple S can still be something." Matthew's eyes turned to the corrals, past them to the clump of aspens with its fresh mound of earth. "It's what he'd have wanted."

Jim bolted from the sound of his father's voice. The faltering hope and acceptance flayed him, poured salt on already aching sores. Even with all his good intentions, could he live up to that hope and make it reality? His steps turned unerringly toward Jon's grave. The simple headstone that read JIM SUTHERLAND stopped him cold. The next moment he laughed, a dreadful sound. Dead and buried.

He knelt by the mound that was already covered with small flowers and tiny green grass blades, making a coverlet. "With God as my witness, Jon, I'll try and take care of the folks and Mescal the way you'd have done." A slight rustle behind him froze him to the spot. Mescal's voice said, "We thought it better to do it this way, in case anyone ever looked at the grave."

Jim slowly turned and met her intent look. "It's a strange feeling, seeing your name on a headstone." His attempt at lightness was a disaster. "Mescal, will you help me?"

He could see her spirit flee before she asked, "How?"

"I don't know much about the Bible. I thought if I give it out I'm spending the next few months getting the place in shape, then plan to study this winter, I can get by until spring before folks pester me to preach. Could you help me study? I hate reading; you know that."

She didn't answer for a full minute. One golden gleam had returned to her eyes, but never had he seen her so subdued. Even the simple blue shirt she wore looked faded and worn. "I'll help you, but can you go through with it? When spring comes, will you really stand before folks and preach?"

"I'll have to." The little grove had turned cold. Jim shivered in the warm day and wondered why life had to be lived at all. Everything preyed on something else. Man on animals. Wolves on rabbits. Mountain lions on deer. Yet only when man preyed on man were the laws of nature broken. Animals killed for food, man for greed or power. Now in order to survive, he was forced to play a different type of game, and one he despised.

Jim played that game all the rest of summer, into the fall. As he feared, Comstock had regained his boldness once away from the Triple S. While not much stock disappeared, and that could be attributed to natural wandering for graze, ugly rumors of persistent attacks on other ranchers and lone riders continued. By the time autumn rode the trails, with its golden showers of colored leaves, everyone for miles around Daybreak was keyed to fever pitch. Men slept with loaded rifles and pistols in easy reach. Those who had anything worth stealing kept it buried or locked up. Herds were moved closer in when possible. Still the outbreak of terror went on, and Mescal never rode alone. Apache faithfully shadowed her if she left the immediate area of ranch buildings.

"Something has to break soon," Jim told Apache one glorious afternoon. They'd ridden out to see where the outfit was in rounding up and tallying strays. "I've let Comstock go his way, hoping he'd get so tangled up in his schemes he'd hang himself, but the whole country's ready to fight at the drop of a hat. I'm not even sure how many of our own hands are loyal."

"Slim, Dave, Shorty, and Red."

"How do you know?" Jim couldn't keep surprise from his voice.

"Apaches have — ways." The slight smile that always accompanied Apache's confessed eavesdropping disappeared. "The others are like the wind in the aspen leaves, tossed about and up for the taking."

Depressed, Jim rode on. "That's four plus you and Dad and me. Not enough if we get a big raid."

"Better to stop the raid before it happens."

Jim's lip curled with some of his old arrogance. "Any ideas?"

"One." Apache shrugged. "You might not want to do it."

"I'm desperate enough to try almost anything." Jim gazed across the land he loved so well, automatically noting the dying of the year. "Shall we round up everything and sell?"

Apache considered a long moment. "That might be good. But it wasn't what I had in mind."

"Well, what was?" Jim's impatience boiled over, a teakettle that had been forced to simmer too long.

"Jon told me once he threatened Radford Comstock with getting himself appointed as sheriff. Comstock showed it hit him hard." Not by an inflection did Apache show it mattered one way or another, but Jim sat up straight from where he'd lounged in the saddle. "You don't mean *me* as sheriff!" He threw back his head, and peal after peal of laughter splintered the autumn air.

Apache didn't even smile. "You asked. I told you." He wheeled King and was gone, leaving Jim alone with the echoes of his own mirth and prey to a host of new thoughts. Time after time he rejected the whole thing as even more insane than his idea of becoming a preacher. What a joke it would be on the Comstocks — Jim Sutherland, whom they'd hung for a crime he hadn't committed, thrust into a position of authority that could break the backbone of their evil deeds.

Although Jim continued to laugh down the idea, the more he thought about it, the more it intrigued him with the possibilities. Meanwhile, the roundup went on. Practically all the stock was sold at top dollar and the money carefully hidden on the Sutherland ranch. "Don't trust it in the bank," Matthew announced. "Too many holdups lately." He personally buried it, refusing to tell the others where it was. "Anything you don't know can't be dug out of you," he insisted. "There are those who know we have a tidy little sum and who wouldn't be above relieving us of it."

Winter swooped with eagle's claws, but the Triple S lay unmolested. With practically all the herd gone and most of the hands off for the winter, an uneasy peace came with the isolation. Jim felt Mescal's eyes on him and wondered. Did she think of the plans and dreams they'd made last winter, before the roaring fire? Or had her show of spunk been for Comstock's benefit only? He couldn't read her eyes, and most of the time she avoided him. Jon's shadow lay between them, ever present, ever real, despite the months since he'd died. When they studied the Bible, there was none of the old teasing that should have gone with it. One late afternoon, when it had grown too dark to study and the older Sutherlands and Apache were in other rooms, Mescal closed the Bible and said, "I don't think you will ever preach, not even one sermon."

"Why?" Jim noted the drooping curl over her left cheek.

"I don't know." Her pensive face caught the fire's glow, and she let her hands lie still in her lap. "It's just a feeling."

"Would you care?" Why had he blurted it out, the first hint he'd let escape that what she thought was of supreme importance to him?

She evaded it. "What will you do, instead?"

"I could become sheriff and clean out the Comstocks."

His random statement turned her face to parchment. "They'd kill you!" She caught the front of his heavy shirt in both hands. Terror shone in her eyes. "Besides, how could Jon Sutherland, learning to be a

235

minister, take the sheriff's job?" She laughed wildly, and her slender body shook. "He couldn't. Daybreak wouldn't stand for it, much as they want and need a new sheriff. They would never let you go against the Comstocks."

Jim caught both hands in his strong ones and pulled her close to him. He could feel the frightened beat of her heart and longed to wrap his arms around her and protect her from any harm, forever. Realization came like a summer storm, quick, unexpected, violent. Months ago he had held her, thought he loved her, looked forward to their being married. It was nothing compared with the sweep of feeling that now rose within him. In one heartbeat Jim saw his former love for what it was: selfish, demanding, a boy's careless asking for a priceless gift.

He drew a dazed breath. A man loved differently. The desire to protect, give, love overrode carelessness in the age-old way of creation of man seeking his mate.

Mescal's fists pounding against his chest and the realization she had mistaken his silence for argument brought him back to the firelit room. Tears chased each other down her cheeks as she repeated, "Jon Sutherland cannot be sheriff. Don't you understand?"

Light through darkness. Lightning in the fog. A rainbow in the rain. Enlightenment, sacrifice, determination. Jim lifted his head, looked above hers into the future. "No —" His jaw set. Jon had gone the last mile; his twin could do no less. *"But Jim Sutherland can."*

12

Jim had once heard a trapped fawn whimper the way Mescal did now. He had freed the spotted animal from a mucky pool and set it back on dry ground. He washed the scratched leg until the water ran clear, and the fawn limped away. But Mescal was no fawn. She was a living, breathing girl-turning-woman who clung to him. "No! Don't do it, Jim. We'll go away and be married. No one will know or care where we came from. Dad Sutherland will give us some of the cattle money to get started." Her strong arms threatened to destroy him; her pleading undermined his determination.

"I have to do it, Mescal, it's the only way." He inexorably loosened her clinging fingers, led her to a chair, and saw her collapse in its depths. His hands shook when he lit a nearby lamp from a fireplace brand then raised his voice, "Dad, Mom, Apache — will you come in here, please?" Every task he had faced paled into nothingness before the one he now faced: convincing them it was their only chance to survive.

He sternly stamped out of his heart Mescal's solution to run away, knowing he might also be killing any chance of her sticking with him.

"What's wrong, Son?" Matthew's keen eyes missed nothing. "Did you make Mescal cry? And why?" He crossed the room and patted the dark head. Abigail and Apache both glanced at them then at Jim.

"I've just been telling Mescal how to get rid of the Comstocks."

Jim's father burst into great laughter. "Wish you'd tell the rest of us."

"I will." Jim fixed his penetrating gaze on Matthew. "Jim Sutherland is going to be resurrected and take the sheriff's job in Daybreak, at least for a time."

"What?" Matthew roared, his face turning beet red. "After all the planning to get the country to believe you were Jon? It doesn't make sense. No wonder Mescal's upset, you young hothead!"

"It makes all the sense in the world." Jim unfolded the plan he'd been making ever since Apache mentioned Jon's threat. "Once folks around here know their crooked sheriff hung *the wrong man* in his little game of covering his own tracks, they'll want something done about it."

"But what about your being in the gang? You think they're just going to overlook that? Or do you think Comstock'll keep his mouth shut?" Matthew pounded a big fist against the arm of Mescal's chair.

Jim hesitated a moment to find words that could cross the throbbing barrier of his heart. Every day of his life had aimed toward this minute. He must make them accept it. "I intend to tell them myself." For the first time he tore himself free from the locked gaze with his father and shifted so he faced them all. As long as he lived he'd remember Mescal's contorted face, his mother's eyes, Apache's suddenly glowing countenance.

"When the snow lifts, we'll ask all the ranchers here for a secret meeting. We'll invite a few of those from Daybreak we know we can trust. I intend to make a clean breast of it and ask for a second chance so I can do something with the Comstocks and make this a fit place for women and children." His soul flamed into his speech. "I tried being Jon, and it didn't work. One thing good came from it. When Jon took my place, I realized Jesus had done the same thing a long time ago. I decided if He — and Jon — cared that much, I had to accept it."

He saw gladness fill his mother's face. "But in spite of all that, I can't take Jon's place, and I don't think he'd want me to. Did you know he was ready to give up everything and fight, if he had to?" Needles poked into Jim's eyelids, and he found he was having trouble breathing.

"There is another way." Apache's voice intruded into Jim's ringing ears. "I can sneak in at night and kill Radford Comstock and maybe some of his relatives. The rest might take warning."

"You'd do that for us?" Jim choked, suddenly feeling Apache had grown to giant proportions.

"Apache pays his debts." The troubled months since Jon's death faded. Jim knew he was again the comrade he'd become after he and Apache shared the burning hell of imprisonment long ago. He gripped Apache's hand but shook his head.

"No. It would only bring the others forward, or worse, put them into hiding. They'd kill from cover. Don't you see?" he appealed to the others, who silently stood a little apart. "It's the only way."

"I can forbid it." The patriarch of the clan's deep voice rolled into the stillness.

"Don't do it, Dad!" Jim dropped Apache's hand and spread his own wide. "I hoped never again to go against you, but even if you order me out of your house, I have to do this last thing I know is right." He threw out the challenge with sinking heart. What lay ahead would be rough. Without his father's backing, it would be worse.

"Stubborn mule! Son of Thunder! How could I have raised such a one?" Matthew Sutherland foamed at the mouth.

Deep insight crept into Jim's feverish brain. He seized his father's mighty arm. "Dad, if it were you in the same place, *wouldn't you do the same thing?*"

Appalled by his daring, but unwilling to take back the cry, Jim watched the storm rise, break, and rage until his father thundered, "Yes! You know I don't hold with killing, but God forgive me, *yes!*" His big eyes rolled. "If it hadn't been for Mother and Mescal and Jon holding me back, I'd probably be out there with him now." He motioned through the snow-draped window to the lonely mound.

Jim knew he had won, but at what cost! Never had his father turned his heart inside out before. Jim instinctively knew he never would again, but for this moment the naked truth shimmered and danced in the room, a fragile but unbreakable strand that bound them together.

"It's settled, then." Matthew's great gulps of air sounded loud. Mescal and Abigail had turned to each other, silently crying. Apache remained where he stood during the conversation, a softness in his look Jim had not seen before.

There was nothing of softness in any of them, weeks later, when the snow began to melt and trails became passable. Matthew and Jim made quiet visits to selected neighbors and ranchers, setting a time for their secret meeting. A full score arrived one afternoon, ate heartily of the excellent supper served, and crowded around the fireplace.

"Some of you are wondering why you're here," Matthew boomed. "No use stalling. It's time the Comstocks were run out of the country."

"Agreed," a lanky rancher cut through the low rumble of assent. "But how're we goin' to do it? Any one of us leaves our place, it gets robbed."

"If we had a new sheriff, things could be mighty different," Matthew cautiously suggested. Jim noticed the way the visitors' faces lighted.

"Shore, but who's goin' to be fool enough to take it away from Radford and get killed for his trouble?" the same rancher inquired.

"My son."

In the quivering stillness Jim heard the hiss of indrawn breath, followed by uneasy shifting of men's bodies. Neither drowned the music in his father's words. They would sing in Jim's ears all through the messy business that lay ahead.

Before anyone could ask the question hovering on everyone's lips, Matthew said, "I've got a story to tell. I ask you to listen without interrupting; then you can have your say."

"Fair enough," several mumbled.

"You all know the Comstocks hanged a son of mine last year." Matthew's voice hardened. "Since then Radford confessed to my other son, Mescal, and Apache, who's been the best friend we could ask for, he made a mistake and that Jim Sutherland wasn't even in on the raid. It came out Jim joined up with the Comstocks in the mistaken idea he'd be helping us. He did succeed in getting our stock and horses back. It doesn't excuse him riding with the gang, but he was wild, you all know that."

"Too bad he got hanged — we could use him right now," someone called.

Matthew's face shone. "Carter, do you mean that?"

Jim could feel his nails digging into his palms and sweat start under his shirt collar. Everything depended on Carter's answer — and the way the others replied.

"Yeah." Beefy, belligerent, Carter leaned forward. "Long's he hadn't killed anybody an' was willin' to help get back what I lost, it'd tickle my funny bone to have Jim Sutherland walk in."

"That goes for me, too," someone else called, but a third said, "What's the use us talkin' about a dead man? He ain't here, is he? He's out there right now." Silence fell as the man beckoned outside.

It was time. The hands of life's clock had ticked off the past, and the present demanded action. Jim stepped forward from the back of the room, where he'd been a silent bystander. "Men, Jim Sutherland isn't dead. *Comstock's outfit hanged the wrong twin!*"

The scrape of someone's boot sounded like an explosion. Taking advantage of the stunned condition of the crowd, Jim said, "I was trussed up, ready to be hanged. My brother Jon came. Knocked me out cold and pitched me through a window. I woke up wearing Jon's shirt and jacket." He felt a pulse beat hard in his temple. "Jon was dead; he'd passed himself off as me so I could go on living." He tried to clear the obstruction in his throat, forced himself to go on. "I went crazy, decided to kill myself. Apache and Mescal saved me — again — him by despising me and calling me a coward, Mescal by believing in me.

"Out in a God-forsaken canyon, I decided to square things to Jon by taking his place, becoming a preacher the way he wanted to do. I can't. I'd be a hypocrite. But I can be a new *Jim* Sutherland." He noted the paralyzed state of his audience. "Apache told me Jon once threatened to run Comstock out of office and take the job himself. At first it seemed insane. Then I saw it was the only thing to do. If you'll give me a second chance, let me do what Carter said and repay you for what I helped take, as soon as I can get the money, just maybe we can get rid of the Comstocks — for good." He could feel his knees start to buckle and grabbed the mantel for support. "I never was in on the killing."

"No one'll have to wait for money, either," Matthew promised. "I can settle up right now, with the roundup money."

Carter finally stood, looming large in the crowd. "Reckon we'd like to talk it over without you here, Matthew. Take Jim outside and wait."

Jim stumbled through the door and into

the kitchen. Mescal met him with out-stretched hands, a terrible question on her lips. "At least they're talking about it," he told her and his mother.

"Thank God for that." Abigail pushed her hair back with a soapy hand, from behind the mountain of dishes she and Mescal had been doing. They lapsed into waiting. One minute. Two. Five. Ten. Then, "Come in here," Carter ordered them curtly. Jim swept the room with a lightning glance. His heart dropped at the expressionless faces, but rested on Apache's. Was that a slight smile?

"Jim Sutherland, are you willin' to uphold law an' order, even if it means bein' killed in doin' it?" Carter demanded.

"I am." A world in a whisper, a second chance.

"Then you're our new sheriff, on one condition — you go after Radford Comstock now, an' we all go with you, every last man of us. We figure he an' his outfit may take a mite of convincin'." Carter's ruddy face split into a broad grin. "I ain't never ridden with an Apache before, but I'm aimin' to now, if he's willin'."

Jim saw the quickly concealed look of amazement in Apache's face as he said, "I will ride." Moments later Matthew Sutherland burst into the room, a heavy sack dangling from one hand. "Before we go, I'll just settle up."

"Nothin' to settle," Carter announced. "That's how come we took so long. You've done given one son an' may have to give another. None've us as what's done that much." He brushed aside Matthew's protests and shoved open the door. "All right, men, ride!"

Jim ran for Shalimar, Apache for King. Matthew saddled Dark Star. A few minutes later the new sheriff and his deputized posse gathered by the front porch.

"I'll be waiting, Jim." Mescal's low voice carried to the mounted men.

Carter said, "Reckon that's enough to get him through!" And the others laughed. One called, "If he don't come back, I will," but there was no insult in the sally, and Mescal smiled tremulously, then slipped back inside. In a body the men rode down the trail and headed for Daybreak, Jim at their head.

"Apache," he turned to his comrade riding abreast of him. "What's the best way to handle things?"

Apache never hesitated. His hands spread in an expansive gesture. "Have some slip in unseen. Let the town people go in naturally. Give the order to wait five minutes until you, your father, and I get to the saloon or sheriff's office — Radford'll probably be at the saloon. When we meet him," a cold smile twisted the thin lips, "you'll know what to do."

Jim gave the orders as stated. It was just before midnight when they reached town, a black, cheerless night well-suited to their errand. Men would die; how many they didn't know. Some of them, some Comstocks. "God," Jim prayed. "If only the wholesale massacre can be avoided." A deep ache inside made him wonder — was the sickness threatening to overwhelm him the same thing Jon experienced that other night?

"Apache, is there any chance we can keep it from being a slaughter?"

Only the voice in the darkness proclaimed Apache still rode near. Vicious clouds had totally obscured the moon and stars, and a dark velvet blanket muffled even the sounds of the posse.

"Perhaps. It all depends on Comstock."

And then they were there, in place. Matthew, Apache and Jim dismounted behind an empty building and dropped their reins. Step by careful step they went until Apache stopped them. "Wait here!" He was gone no more than a minute. "Sheriff's office is empty. They're in the saloon." When they reached the crouching building, Apache grunted. "Good — not many horses." Again he left them, scouted, returned. "Radford Comstock, six of his gang, a bartender, two town drunks off to one side."

Jim's heart leaped. Chances were slim the Comstocks would surrender without a fight, but it was not impossible.

"Stay outside the window until your eyes can stand the light," Apache cautioned. Jim blessed him for the thought. The moment he changed from dark night to brightly lighted room his eyes betrayed him. He blinked several times, and his vision cleared.

"Now!" Apache whispered in his ear.

A board creaked under Jim's foot as he crossed the rude porch floor. There must be no time for warning. He burst through the doors, revolvers in both hands. "Up with them!" He could hear his father's breathing over his shoulder, feel Apache's arm graze his as he pushed to one side.

Radford Comstock leaned his chair back, a sardonic smile on his face. "Well, if it ain't the preacher!"

"Not the preacher." Jim flipped one revolver the way he'd done in camp and was rewarded by Comstock's scrambling to his feet, craven face etched in horror.

"I hanged you!" The damning confession bounced off bottles and tables, and the men around Comstock leaped to one side, leaving him alone to face his ghost.

"You hanged my brother." Jim's strident voice turned Comstock's face even more ashen. "For a crime not even I was in on."

"Yes, yes." Comstock was beyond reason. "But there were other times. . . ."

"We know all about them, an' about you." Carter's authoritative voice came from the door at the back. He and a half-dozen other heavily armed ranchers pushed their way in. "Now we've decided we're goin' to have a new sheriff."

Jim saw the moment knowledge he was finished sank into Radford Comstock's brain. He raised his shaking hands. "I'll leave, get out of the country. My men'll go with me." His dirty-gray face shook.

"Better make it a long way out," Jim suggested in a soft, chilling voice. "We could hang you right here and be perfectly legal."

Comstock shot him a venom-drenched look but said nothing.

"We'd just as soon not have your dirty blood on this town's conscience. Get out!"

251

Jim threw wide the doors and waited until the last of the men were outside. Under close guard they were hustled onto their horses and driven down the inky street, cursing all the way. They headed out, and Jim felt his screaming muscles unknot. "Not a shot fired!"

He spoke too soon. From the pitch darkness a single explosion came. Jim was half lifted from his saddle, spun around and fell.

"Son!" Matthew was beside him. "You all right?"

Fire ran down Jim's left shoulderblade. He reached toward it. "It's high."

"Thank God!" Matthew caught his son in his arms and took long strides toward the doctor's home. "Apache, run ahead and tell Doc I'm —" but Apache had disappeared. "Gone after them," Matthew muttered.

"Not alone!" Jim cried. "They're seven to one!"

"Naw, the rest of the posse's followed them." Matthew stayed with Jim while Doc removed a bullet, poured whiskey in the wound until Jim thought he'd shriek, and bandaged it tightly.

"Don't s'pose there's any use tellin' you to take it easy," Doc said sourly, and Jim laughed. "What good's a brand-new sheriff who lets his posse go after a gang of outlaws without him?" He swung his feet to the floor, clutched his spinning head with his right arm, and fell back.

"Told you so." Doc seemed to get a grim satisfaction from his awkwardness and shoved him back down on the table. A little later he helped Jim to a narrow cot but wouldn't let him get up. "What's left of tonight will at least give you a head start on healin'," he said. But neither Matthew nor Jim got any sleep. Somewhere out in the night men battled not only for life, but for the right to live free of fear. With all their hearts they longed to be there.

A disturbed dawn broke, and Jim could be restrained no longer. He struggled into his boots and with his father made his way outside. The slow steps of tired horses nailed him to the ground. The posse had returned. Haggard faces and a significant shape on one of the horses' backs told the story. Jim searched the group. "Apache?"

Carter, all red gone from his heavy face, stepped forward. "Gone. We caught up with them and were all for hangin' them. Apache said no. He said you didn't want killin'. We covered him, an' he checked the guns to see which had been fired. When he got to Radford, the fool grabbed for his gun and shot Apache." Carter's mouth twisted. "Rest of us were so stupid we couldn't move. Apache jerked Comstock off his horse, fightin' every inch, an' headed for a tree. I flipped my rope over a limb, an' Comstock went loco. Never saw anyone so strong." Carter wiped his sweaty face, and Jim's nerves shrilled. "Turned his own gun on himself."

"But Apache!" Jim cried.

"Said to tell you the debt was paid, whatever that means, an' he reckoned you wouldn't care if he took King. He rode off, saggin' in the saddle, spite of all we could do."

Matthew leaped for Dark Star, patiently standing near. "We'll go after him. Bring him back. He can't die out there alone."

Out there. Jim bit back a sob. Sullen red walls. Parched earth. Barren miles. A waterfall. Desert voices, whispering, echoing with final understanding. "It's what he wants. He'll die alone or maybe heal as I did." Love for the tragic mixture of white and red blood filled his farseeing eyes with sand. "Maybe, someday. . . ." A vision of a plodding figure on a powerful gray horse crossed his vision and disappeared.

Carter and the posse fell back. Matthew

254

didn't speak for a long time. Tragedy hovered too near, too red. When he did, it was gruff. "Can you ride? Mother and Mescal will be waiting."

Jim looked north and east once more. "I can ride." He wet dry lips and called Shalimar. The debt *had* been paid — in full.

About the Author

Colleen L. Reece spent her childhood reading the novels of Zane Grey and vowed one day to write westerns. *Voices in the Desert* and *Echoes in the Valley* are the realization of that childhood vow.